Tangled Temptation

Marie Tuhart

Hot Blooded Press

TANGLED TEMPTATION

QUALITY CONTROL: We strive to produce error-free books, but even with all the eyes that see the story during the production process, slips get by. So please, if you find a typo or any formatting issues, please let us know at marie@marietuhart.com so that we may correct it.

Thank you!

Blurbs

♥

Angie Davidson never expected to feel so adrift after her best friend's wedding at Quick Silver Ranch. With nothing tying her down and no clear direction, she's restless—until the ranch's brooding, sinfully handsome co-owner catches her eye. Jared Turner is distant, untouchable... until the moment their lips meet, and the world catches fire.

Jared doesn't do attachments, but he can't ignore the way Angie surrenders so perfectly beneath his touch. He offers her a challenge—two weeks to explore the explosive passion simmering between them, no strings attached. He's been burned before, rejected for his brand of desire, and he refuses to let history repeat itself.

But Angie isn't like anyone he's known, and with every stolen moment, every heated night, she burrows deeper under his skin. As desire turns into something neither of them expected, they'll have to decide if taking a risk on love is worth the ultimate surrender.

Acknowledgements

I want to acknowledge the following people:

Laurie, as always you keep me sane.

Red Quill Editing LLC, for all your hard work.

Contents

Chapter One

♥

I'm pathetic. Angie Davidson sat at the table and watched her best friend, Becca, and her husband, Tyler, enjoy the bride and groom dance. It had been six months since Becca's trip to the ranch and reconnecting with Tyler. Quick Silver Ranch never looked more beautiful to her, with the large flower-laden pavilion tents shading the guests from the sun. The place was filled with joy, laughter, and love.

And she was jealous.

Jealous of Becca finding her man, jealous of losing her best friend, and jealous of everyone's happiness. Angie knew that wasn't fair, but it was how she felt. Heck, she was the one who sent Becca to the ranch where she found Tyler, her previous lover.

Angie had spent the last two days at the ranch helping Becca prepare for her wedding. Not that she hadn't enjoyed herself—she had. But with that fun came the realization that her best friend was now living at the ranch, a two-hour drive from her.

Not really far, but there would be no more late-night calls to go out for ice cream, impromptu window shopping, and Angie would be alone in San Francisco. She was truly happy for her friend, very happy, but loneliness had begun to settle in, and she hated it.

She hated it as a kid at the orphanage—until she was adopted. She hated it as a teenager since her adopted brothers were all older. She was always the one standing alone, never picked for anything, and never fitting in. As she got older, she appreciated her adoptive parents and brothers.

At least with Becca, she had a friend she could share a bottle of wine with, go out to the movies or dinner, or just watch chick flicks and cry.

Someone she could discuss sex with and not feel like an outcast.

She forced her gaze from the happy couple and glanced around the pavilion, only to have Jared Turner amble into her line of sight. At six foot two and with an aura of authority, he stood out among the wedding guests in his tux. Maybe *guests* wasn't the right word. Everyone here was an employee of the Quick Silver Ranch except her.

Becca had chosen not to invite her mother—boy, was *that* a long story— and Tyler had no family. Besides, Becca had told Angie the employees of the ranch were her friends, as they had accepted Becca with open arms as the ranch caterer. Angie wondered how it would feel to be part of this special family. Angie hated it when self-pity hit her. She was happy for her friend, but her emotions were a tangled knot in her throat.

Pushing her thoughts away, her gaze traveled over Jared's fine form. She sighed. He was a real man, and he didn't treat her like the indecisive men she'd dated. No. Jared took charge. And it turned her on. Her nipples grew hard every time she saw him.

That was an unusual reaction for her. It was the man himself. In the short time she'd known him, Jared showed the confidence to take anything on. Nothing like the men in her life or at her job. She worked for an accounting firm as an assistant and climbed the company ladder, but somehow along the way, she'd become one of the boys. They all looked to her for decisions and they deferred to her in conversation.

She was tired of it. She wanted a man who would take control, at least for a little while. Jared was the man to do it.

How can I get him to respond to me?

Becca and Tyler were leaving for their honeymoon later today. Angie wasn't expected to return to the city for two weeks. She'd planned it that way. She needed a distraction, something to break her out of this somber mood.

Could I seduce Jared tonight? Well, maybe not quite seduce. The goal was for him to take her to bed and dominate her for the night. She wanted to lie back and enjoy, not do all the work.

A feminine squeal caught her attention, and Angie saw Tyler had dipped Becca low as they danced. Angie grinned. They were so perfect for each other, so in love.

Angie jumped when a masculine hand closed over hers on the table. She tilted her head and saw Jared, his brown eyes twinkling and a grin playing around his sensual lips. Her heart jumped.

Without a word, he pulled her to her feet and out onto the makeshift dance floor.

Yes. Maybe he was attracted to her and maybe seducing him would be easier than she'd thought.

The music had changed. Angie remembered she was the maid of honor, and Jared was the best man; they were required to dance with each other. Her good mood plummeted.

She rested her left hand on his shoulder, and he grasped her right hand, his left hand against her lower back. Blood surged through her veins as they began to waltz. Thank goodness she'd taken dancing lessons years ago. Jared held her close as they danced.

"It's a beautiful wedding," she said and winced at her inane comment.

"Yes." Jared glanced at the couple dancing. "I'm glad I could do something for Becca and Tyler." His voice was whisky smooth.

"They're great together, aren't they?"

"Yes."

Angie stopped talking and drank in the feel of his body against hers as they danced. His hardness to her softness. His hold was the only thing keeping her from melting into a puddle at his feet. She wanted him, so why wasn't she making a move?

Come on, where is that brave, daring woman?

"Becca mentioned you're closing the ranch for a while." She shifted closer to him.

His hand pressed the slightest bit harder on her back as he gazed at her. "Two weeks. We have some renovations to make, and the staff needs some downtime. It works out perfectly with Tyler gone."

"How much can be done in two weeks? When the offices where I work were renovated, it took months." *And the workmen came to me to solve problems instead of senior management.*

"A lot—if you know how to motivate people."

"Oh?" She tilted her head and fluttered her lashes at him, corny, she knew, but hopefully effective. "And how would you do that?"

He grinned. "Lots of money." He shifted so there was less space between their bodies.

Her fingers trailed over his broad shoulders to his neck. She stroked his dark brown hair. His hand tightened on her lower back, bringing their hips together, his erection firm against her, even with their formal clothing. *Yes! Maybe tonight will work out after all.*

Angie skimmed her hand from his neck over his back, fingers dancing against his spine, to his well-defined ass. She rested her palm over one cheek and squeezed.

"Behave." His breath brushed her ear as he swatted her ass.

"You hit me!" *He actually smacked my ass!* Not that it hurt—it hadn't. But now, heat flowed through her veins. How had one little swat made her so hot and needy?

"I'll do worse if you don't behave yourself, Angie."

"Promise?" The word slipped from her before she realized it. The music ended and Jared kept his arm around her waist as he escorted her back to the table and pulled out her chair.

Before she could sit, he cupped her cheeks and tilted her head up. "We'll talk later." He dropped a brief, hard kiss on her lips before he released her and strode away.

Her heart skipped several beats as she watched him cross the room. Her hand rose to her lips as she sank onto the chair. *Oh, yeah.* If he met her later, there wouldn't be any talking.

***

Jared strode across the tent as he struggled to control his libido.

Have I lost my mind? Nope, just control of his libido. Angie was a force to be reckoned with, and he was just the man to take her in hand.

Since the day she'd stepped foot on the ranch, his mind and body reacted. She was beautiful in the classic sense. It amused him when she tried to force her blonde hair into clips and it continually escaped; his dick hardened every time he caught her staring at him with those deep blue eyes.

His reaction to her surprised him. She knew how to use her sex appeal to her full advantage, and he could tell she was used to being in full control, which might be an issue if he continued on the path he wanted.

He'd noticed over the past few days her innate ability to take charge—with the vendors, with Becca, with the ranch staff. Giving orders seemed second nature for Angie.

Would she release that control in the bedroom? Jared shook his head.

His psyche was one of dominance. Unless he could dominate a woman in the bedroom, in their sex life, he couldn't be satisfied. There weren't a lot of women willing to give up total control to a man, even a man they professed to love.

It was very possible Angie couldn't or wouldn't either. He'd have to test her before he took this any further.

But was that the right thing to do? He put his hands in his pockets. Jared hadn't questioned his life choices in a long time.

Something had nagged at the back of his head ever since Tyler and Becca announced their engagement. Something he couldn't quite define but wouldn't go away. And being introduced to Angie hadn't quieted that voice at all.

Tyler was one lucky man to find Becca, a woman who enjoyed his sexual games and didn't mind what they did at the ranch. Jealousy hit Jared hard. He wanted someone like Becca in his life.

A woman who accepted him for who and what he was. Would that ever happen? Not based on his past experiences with women. Most of them thought they could change him or ran from him.

Across the room, Vic, the ranch's chef, wheeled out the wedding cake.

Good. The party was almost over. Once it was done, he would get Angie alone and see how serious she was about wanting more from him. Her single word of *promise* made his dick thicken.

***

An hour later, Jared walked with the happy couple to their waiting vehicle.

"Don't work too hard while we're gone," Becca said, standing on her toes to brush a kiss over his cheek.

"Mind your own business, woman." Jared smiled at Becca. "You are to enjoy your honeymoon and not worry about what I'm doing." He wasn't about to tell Becca about the sensual activities he wanted to do with her best friend. It was better left unsaid.

"We'll enjoy it all right, thanks to you," Tyler said.

Jared waved his hand in dismissal. Yes, he'd paid for the exclusive trip to the Meadowood resort in Napa Valley.

Tyler was his best friend and business partner, and it was the least he could do for the couple.

He stood with the others watching the couple drive away. As the group broke up, he turned and noticed Angie standing not ten feet away. His blood heated. She did that to him. And his cock took notice too.

She lowered those lush lashes before her gaze skimmed down his body to stop at his groin. When their gazes reconnected, he saw the need and raw desire there. Now was the time to deal with Angie and find out what she really wanted.

Her eyes widened as his body pressed against hers. "Yes, or no?" he hoarsely rasped. When she didn't answer. "I'm done playing games."

She trembled slightly against him and he was about to back off when she licked her lips and said, "Yes. Oh yes."

Consent. He leaned down and took her lips with his, thrusting his tongue into her mouth. He tasted the slight sweetness from what he thought was the wedding cake, but probably was Angie's own natural taste. He broke the kiss, and she leaned on him as if she couldn't stand on her own two legs.

Elation filled him. She wasn't running or telling him off. "I'm not like other men." Would she be able to handle his compelling need for dominance?

"I don't want other men. I want you."

"Fine. I understand you have the next two weeks off. You can spend them here, but if you stay, you'll play by my rules. I'll be the one in charge. The rest we can discuss later."

She nodded, her breathing shallow.

"I'll see you in the morning." Jared released her and walked away, his body protesting with every step he took. He had to set the tone of this test and their relationship from the beginning. She'd either turn tail and run or rage at him. Maybe she'd stay, but he doubted it.

It would be interesting to see what she'd do.

Chapter Two

♥

Angie's stomach clenched as Jared walked away. She almost yelled at him to come back, but hesitated. She'd never felt so turned on in her life at his words and his kiss. Her legs were weak and her heart pounded.

Who's seducing who here?

He basically told her what to do and expected her to do it.

And she was considering it. How crazy was that?

She made her way across the compound to her cabin, and once inside, went to the bedroom. She kicked off her shoes, removed her dress, and flopped on the bed in her underwear and stockings.

"So, what *are* you going to do?" she asked herself out loud. "Part of me wants to pack up and leave in the morning."

But another part told her to stay and see just how much she could test Jared's control.

Staring up at the ceiling, she listed out the pros and cons.

Pros meant sex and not feeling so lonely, the cons were whatever other rules he had in mind.

What else? Angie shook her head. "Why am I trying to decide this with cold hard logic? This is all about how I feel. How Jared makes me feel." And damn if he didn't make her feel like a desirable woman.

It sounded almost silly, but it was true. Her body grew hot at a single glance from him. Her nipples were always hard around him. Today, while they danced, her skin tingled, and when they kissed... Those lips could be considered a lethal weapon.

It all hinged on what she wanted to do. Jared told her she'd have to play by his rules, and she had a feeling those rules were going to test her resolve, both physically and sexually. Her pussy clenched with need.

Nothing could be settled now, not with her body trying to override her mind. She rolled off the bed, grabbed her favorite waterproof vibrator from her suitcase, and went into the bathroom. She needed to take the edge off, and then she could make a decision.

***

At nine the next morning, Angie walked into the dining room of the main house. Compared to the last few days, it was quiet. Almost too quiet. She paused. Since most of the staff were leaving for two weeks due to the renovations, the quiet made sense.

"Good morning, Angie," Vic said.

"Morning, Vic." She walked to the sideboard and poured herself a cup of coffee.

"Would you like me to fix you something to eat, or is the cold buffet, okay?"

"I'm fine with the buffet. Aren't you leaving the ranch?"

"No. Kathy and I are staying. We do plan to enjoy ourselves while we've got some time off. Jared's given any staff who stay free run of the ranch."

"Oh." Angie sipped her coffee and sat down. Did having some of the staff around make a difference in her staying? Good question. But before she could think of an answer, Jared walked in.

Her pussy tightened. He wore a black shirt that stretched the fabric to the limit, a pair of black jeans, and black cowboy boots, completing the look of bad boy extraordinaire or master of the ranch.

"Morning, boss."

"Morning, Vic, Angie." He nodded in her direction, but didn't look at her.

"There are sandwiches in the fridge, and dinner is there too. All you have to do is put it in the microwave to heat up."

"Don't you know the meaning of the concept of 'time off'?" Jared asked.

"No, and you don't either." Vic smiled. "But don't worry, you won't see a lot of me or Kathy."

"I better not. Cabin two is all set up for the two of you. Let me know how the new items work out."

Vic rubbed his hands together and called over his shoulder as he was leaving the room, "I can't wait."

While the conversation interested Angie, she kept her attention on her coffee cup. She wasn't sure where this shyness was coming from. Being shy didn't get her what she wanted, but with Jared…

Her stomach roiled. What was it about him that made her revert to that shy six-year-old?

"Angie."

She looked up to find Jared's piercing gaze focused on her.

"I'm having your clothing and belongings moved from your cabin to the third floor here in the main house."

Angie almost spewed her coffee. "That's a big assumption you're making there."

"You're here." He leaned against the sideboard, legs crossed, cradling a mug in his hands, watching her with those deep brown eyes. No one would ever accuse him of having puppy dog eyes. No, his were deep and mysterious.

"Maybe I wanted breakfast before I left."

He shrugged. "Fine. You've got ten minutes." His firm voice sent shivers up her spine.

"Ten minutes?"

"I'm going out onto the back porch. You have ten minutes to follow me. It's up to you what you do, but know this: If you follow me, your actions will confirm your consent. If you don't, no harm, no foul." He drained his mug and set it down before leaving.

Her mouth fell open. He'd walked away from her again. She hated it when people walked away from her before she was finished with them. She wouldn't allow it. If anyone left, it would be her. And *no* man walked away before she was finished.

Ever.

Rising, she fought her anger and followed him outside. Food could wait. "We still have things to discuss." The tightness in her voice made her legs quiver.

"Right now, there's nothing to discuss. That you're here tells me you've made your decision."

Before she could react to his words, she found herself pinned against the house, his lips on hers, and she melted into his embrace.

His lips were firm and demanding. No asking, just taking. His tongue thrust between her lips, seeking her tongue. Without thought, she tangled her tongue with his, dueling with him, fighting for control.

Jared broke the kiss and stared down at her. "Stop topping from the bottom."

"What are you talking about?"

"You'll see." He captured her lips once again.

Her brain shut down, and her body filled with heat and need. She didn't fight Jared as he took over.

***

Elation hit Jared when he took control of the kiss and she let go of her control and submitted. He'd been right about Angie. She wanted a man to take control, and he was the man to do it. It wasn't arrogance; it was knowledge. As a sexual psychologist, he'd learned to read the most subtle of signals.

He was grateful she wore a button-down shirt and a flowing skirt. It would make things much easier and more fun. He broke the kiss and rested his forehead against hers. Angie's chest rose and fell with her rapid breathing.

"Today, we will talk. If you're still here in the morning, then I'll know you've accepted my terms."

Yes, he was giving her another out. He had to. They hadn't discussed anything, and he wouldn't keep a woman without her full consent. Angie needed to know what she was getting into.

She crossed her arms over her chest and huffed. "Haven't I already agreed by staying today? And I did let you kiss me."

"I've rushed things. I want your full consent about what we will be doing while you're here. I don't want you saying I lied or didn't tell you something. Please have a seat." He gestured to the two heavy wicker chairs.

Angie sauntered over and sat.

He followed at a leisurely pace. "Understand this: I'm a Dominant through and through. If you stay, you will have to accept that."

"In the bedroom?" He heard a note of uncertainty in her voice.

"In all matters of sex and sensuality." He placed his palms on his thighs. "That includes other places besides the bedroom.

Goose bumps rose on her arms, and her hips shifted ever so slightly.

Ahh, she likes the idea.

"I can accept your dominance in the bedroom and other areas."

Triumph surged through him before he pushed it down. There was still more they needed to get through. "I will use toys and orgasm denial."

She nodded. "I want a safe word."

His eyebrows rose. She wasn't uneducated about BDSM. Interesting, but not totally surprising. She'd sent Becca here, but Becca insisted Angie hadn't known what type of place Quick Silver was. *Had Angie lied to Becca, or did she research after Becca told her?*

"I would never scene without one."

"Good."

"Communication is important. If you're feeling uncomfortable in any position I put you in, if you feel pain, or there is something you absolutely don't want to do, you must use your safe word. Nothing else will make me stop." He paused, but all she did was nod. "You will tell me how I'm making you feel at all times. If you're scared. If you're uneasy. I want to know I'm turning you on, making you hot, or when you're about to climax."

Her hips shifted. He had a feeling she was turned on. *Very good.* She was responsive to him, and they hadn't even started yet. But he knew she would respond to him, she had already.

"Your safe word is *red* to stop, *yellow* to slow down, and *green* if all is good."

"Got it."

"Let's start." Her head jerked up when he spoke. He wasn't planning to do anything yet. He needed her full attention, plus he wanted to be sure she'd keep her word.

"I—"

"Be quiet." Her eyes widened at his firm tone, but he gave her credit, she didn't say a word. "I want you to remove your bra."

She swallowed, and her eyes fluttered shut.

Jared sat back to give her room and waited. When she didn't move, he continued. "You've got one minute. Beyond that and you'll be punished."

"You didn't say anything about punishment."

Jared groaned. "I didn't, but should have." Angie had a way of making him forget to finish up his protocols. "I expect you to do what I tell you to do. If you don't want to, simply say you're safe word and we can discuss or move on." He paused to let the words sink in. "If you don't use your safe word, and don't do as I have directed, there will be punishment."

"And what would that entail?"

"A spanking for the first couple of infractions. After that we'll discuss if it happens." He doubted it would take more than a spanking or two with her.

Angie took a deep breath. "All right."

"Remove your bra." He kept his gaze on her face. He couldn't detect any distress, only excitement. Normally, he'd talk more with his submissive, finding out her likes and dislikes. With Angie, he didn't want to take the time to wait. He wanted her now. This woman was a temptation.

She pulled her shirt from her skirt, then curved her arms around her back, underneath her shirt. He enjoyed the way the shirt tightened against her breasts. The next thing he knew, she was drawing her bra straps down her arms under the fabric and pulling off her bra without removing her shirt.

Clever girl. Admiration filled him. He'd underestimated her. All his instructions would have to be explicit and detailed. Angie was determined to retain some control.

With her bra dangling from her finger she waited.

"Take your panties off."

Color flooded her cheeks, but she didn't hesitate. She dropped her bra and managed to remove her underwear without showing him anything but a small amount of leg. Angie dropped them on top of her bra next to the chair.

"How many men have you had sex with?" He leaned back in his chair.

"I'm twenty-eight, not eighteen. How the hell do I know?"

"I'm thirty-two, and I've had sex with fifteen women. How many?"

"Fifty." Her sarcastic tone came through loud and clear.

While he admired her fire, she needed to learn about submitting to him.

"Unbutton your blouse."

Her hands didn't budge.

"If you won't obey me, this is over." He stood, disappointed she couldn't take such a simple order from him.

"Damn bossy man," she muttered as she unbuttoned her shirt.

"I'm the man you need." When she finished, her breathing was rapid. "Now open it and bare your tits to me."

Her fingers trembled as she followed his directions, glancing around. She was nervous because they were outside, and he looked forward to showing her the sensuality of bare skin, open air, and him. Jared stood, walked behind her chair, and gazed down at her bare chest. Magnificent pale globes. Her breasts rose unsteadily as she tried to calm her breathing.

"Have you ever been tied up?" He returned to his chair. The view from there was even better. Her nipples were taut.

"No." Her tongue darted out and touched her lips.

He would be the first to teach her bondage. A pleasant thrill coursed through him. "How many different positions have you had sex in?"

She lowered her lashes. "Two."

Angie kept surprising him. With her confidence, he figured she was more adventurous in the bedroom.

Apparently, he was wrong.

"Missionary and..." he prompted.

"Doggie."

"None of your lovers has ever taken you up against a wall, in a chair, spread eagled on the floor, bent over the back of the sofa?" Damn if he wasn't growing hard thinking about taking her in all those positions.

He almost missed her answer, her voice was so quiet. "No."

"Your lovers were not very imaginative, were they?"

"Which is why I never got off with them." Angie clapped a hand over her mouth.

Jared grinned. *So, the truth comes out.* In a way, it pleased him that he would be the first to give her mind-blowing orgasms.

She dropped her hand. "Tell me I didn't say that out loud."

"Can't do that, but I'm glad you did. We have to be honest with each other. I will always be honest with you, and I expect the same." He rested his elbows on his knees. "What kind of toys do you use?"

"A vibrator." Her fingers tightened on the wicker chair. She wasn't comfortable with this, and he had to wonder why. He wasn't really pushing her, just getting information he needed.

"What else?"

"I don't think—"

"Answer me." He wouldn't let her get away with avoiding his questions.

She swallowed. "A dildo and nipple clamps."

His dick jumped at the thought of her nipples adorned by clamps and her pussy filled with one of his toys. "Did you like the clamps?"

She nodded.

"Do you like to suck a man?" If she didn't, they'd talk about it. He enjoyed having a woman's lips wrapped around his cock.

"It depends."

"On?"

"The man I'm with."

Her eyes were clear, and she was staring at him. She was being honest. "Do you like having your pussy licked?"

"Yes. If it's done right."

"Oh, I'll do it right." He leaned closer to her. "Is your pussy wet?"

"Yes." Her eyes widened, and Jared realized she didn't mean to say that out loud. *I'm going to have so much fun with her.*

"Spread your legs and show me how wet you are."

"What if someone walks by?"

"No one will. We're in the back, and what's a little fun without the chance of being caught? Spread those legs."

Angie shifted before she grabbed her skirt and lifted it until he could see her pubic hair. The chair wasn't wide enough for what he wanted. He stood, grabbed the pillows off another chair and walked behind Angie.

"Slide down until your ass rests on the edge of the chair."

She bit her lip but adjusted her position, her hands gripping the arms of the chair and keeping her back straight.

Jared placed one pillow behind her back. "Relax against the pillow." He put a second one on the chair. "Let your head rest against this one."

Her head arched back. He leaned over and brushed a soft kiss over her lips before returning to his chair. He pushed his seat closer, then pressed her legs outward until he could see her glistening pussy.

He was a little surprised she offered no resistance. It was good she was turning control over to him.

"Beautiful." Her clit swelled with excitement. *I wonder how she'll taste.* That would have to wait. He had more questions for her. "Have you ever had anal sex?"

"Ummm...no."

"Do you want to try?"

Her legs tensed. "I'm not sure." Her breathing was coming in small pants. "I tried a butt plug once, but it was painful."

"Then you didn't do it right. I'll make sure you're ready before we try, and I promise it won't hurt. Maybe burn a little, but very little pain. Have any of your lovers spanked you?"

She giggled. "I haven't been spanked since I was a child. Unless you count that swat you gave me last night."

"How did the swat make you feel?" Her ass had been firm under his palm. Anticipation of warming those cheeks filled him with need.

"Hot."

"Have you ever experienced impact play with implements or floggers?"

"I'm not into pain."

"Neither am I. There are ways to make a spanking or flogging feel good." Jared made mental notes. Her legs were beginning to quiver. "You can sit up now but lift your skirt and sit your bare ass on the cushion. Keep the fabric above your waist so I can see you."

To his surprise, she never hesitated and followed his orders. Pleasure coursed through him. His instincts were right, Angie was a natural submissive.

"Ever been with another woman?" he asked.

"Hell, no. And don't even think about it."

He chuckled at her reply. "All right, no other women. What about two or more men?"

"Two or more?" Her eyes widened. "I've thought about two men, but not more than that."

He rubbed his chin. *So, she'd thought about a threesome. Interesting.* Jared glanced at his watch. Damn, he had to meet the construction crew in fifteen minutes. Time flew around Angie.

"That's enough for today."

"What?" Angie shook her head.

"Our first session is concluded."

"Oh." She didn't move and looked confused.

"I will never hurt you. I might push you, demand things from you that you don't think you can give, but I will never deliberately harm you. You are precious gift to me, one I intend to see is given pleasure."

She blinked. "Jared—"

He held up his hand. "Meet me in my office at one; we'll have lunch." He stood. "We'll talk about your fantasies, and I want to hear every little detail, because I'm going to make those fantasies come true."

With that, he turned and walked away. If he didn't get out of there now, he might stick his rock-hard dick into her pussy, and that would defeat everything. He wanted her to know he was the one in control, not the other way around.

Whoever said the sub had all the power knew what they were talking about.

***

Angie sat there watching Jared walk away yet again. Her stomach clenched tighter with his every step. Her bones felt like jelly, and her body was on fire, her pussy pulsing with need. All that from him talking to her and staring at her body.

I'm in trouble.

A grin curled her lips. This was the kind of trouble she would enjoy. Forcing herself to move, she picked up her bra and panties, folded them, and made her way back inside the main house. Well, now the place she was staying. Unless her stuff hadn't been moved yet. She climbed the stairs to the third floor to confirm before she walked to her cabin.

Only one door on the entire floor stood open, and she saw her things inside the room. Jared worked fast. Angie unpacked, grateful for something to do. But she couldn't get Jared's last words out of her head. He wanted every detail about her fantasies.

Could she tell him her most intimate secrets? Things not even Becca knew about? Flopping on the bed, she stared at the ceiling, trying to figure out how much she would share with Jared.

She'd always considered her fantasies private. It came from growing up in an orphanage where she had no privacy. After she was adopted, she gained some privacy but had two nosy big brothers, so she'd never even written those imaginings in a diary.

Her fantasies centered around men staying with her and not leaving like all the other men in her life. *Should I share them with Jared?* Maybe. Because deep down, she already wanted to share everything with him, and that scared her.

She'd never shared her feelings of abandonment with any-one. In all honesty, as turned on as she was, she still didn't know.

Maybe I should reconsider staying.

Chapter Three

♥

In Jared's office later, Angie pushed her food around on her plate. She couldn't eat. Hell, she couldn't think. No, that wasn't quite right. She'd been thinking too much. For the last hour and a half in her bedroom, she'd fought with herself. Stay or leave.

But she hadn't been able to get off the mattress and start packing. She wasn't one to walk away from a challenge, but wasn't it better to walk now before Jared could abandon her like other men had? Hadn't she had enough rejection in her life?

"Not hungry?" he asked.

"Not really." She pushed her plate away and noticed Jared's plate was clean. Her thoughts chased themselves around in her mind, making her more confused and unsure. She hated feeling unsure of herself.

"If you're finished," he said as he rose to his feet. "We'll drop these dishes in the kitchen and then go outside."

Decision time.

She picked up her plate and frowned when it shook in her hand. She wasn't scared— apprehensive maybe—so why was she shaking? How would Jared take her fantasies? Would he condemn her for them?

They dropped their plates in the kitchen, then were on the back porch. Jared led her over to a pair of lounging chairs and faced her. "What is bothering you?"

She stared at him. "I'm fine." She crossed her arms over her chest, not willing to give anything away. Hell, she still hadn't decided or had she? After all, she'd unpacked all her things and put them away.

"You didn't eat breakfast or lunch. You're stiff as a board and, while I like your spunk, something is not right." He grasped her shoulders. "If you're worried about me walking away before I fuck you, teach you, dominate you, don't be. I'm looking forward to this."

How did he read my mind? Damn if her pussy didn't pulse at his words. *I should tell him I'm leaving. But I really don't want to.* There was nothing that said she had to tell him everything. She pushed away her doubts and made her decision. *I'm staying.* If she didn't explore what Jared offered her, she'd always wonder what might have been.

"Play time." He rubbed his hands together. The words caused her to close her eyes, but her body reacted to the word. Her gut tightened, and her nipples grew hard.

"Did you put your panties back on?"

"No." A quiver worked its way up her spine. It hadn't made sense to put them back on when she knew he'd have her take them off again.

"Good. Remove your skirt, lie down on the lounger, and let your legs dangle over the sides."

Biting her lower lip, Angie slipped off her skirt. A cool breeze brushed over her sensitive skin as she walked to the lounger and arranged herself. God, she felt so exposed with her legs spread like this, but so ready for Jared.

He circled around her and flashed a grin. Angie's insides melted at his pleasure in her obedience. He leaned over and brushed a light kiss across her lips.

"You are stunning," he said.

She opened her mouth to thank him, but her words dried up as he whipped off his T-shirt.

Holy shit. This man had muscles over muscles. Well-defined pecs begged for her touch...

And talk about a six-pack...

Jared didn't strike her as a gym rat. No, this man earned his physique from working the ranch.

He pushed the other lounger toward her and frowned. "Put your right leg back on your lounger." Once she did that, he pushed his lounger next to hers and reclined. Jared reached over, lifted her leg and placed it over his. "That's better."

Angie bit her lip. In this position, she was wide open to whatever he wanted to do. And it made her feel sexy.

"Before we start, are you having any second thoughts about staying?" He ran his fingers over her upper thigh.

Tingles swept over her skin as she shook her head.

He arched an eyebrow. "Words."

"No second thoughts." Maybe third, fourth, and fifth, but no second. She wouldn't allow herself to have any more doubts about what she was doing. Her reaction to Jared might cause her some apprehension, but her body wanted this.

"Good. Tell me your first fantasy."

"What makes you think I have more than one?"

"Because you do." His brown eyes twinkled. "Lots of women like to fantasize, and so do men."

"Do you?"

"Yes."

"Will you tell me one of yours first?" What were his fantasies like?

He shifted position and stayed silent. Disappointment shot through her. If she had to share, it would only be fair if he did, right? Maybe she was expecting too much, as always.

"After being out here this morning with you…" he started, his voice low, "…seeing you aroused and needy, you haven't left my thoughts. The entire time I was with the construction crew, I thought about you. How beautiful you are. This afternoon, I had the vision of you on the lounger, your arms tied over your head, your legs restrained and… You're shaking."

"Yes." Tremors swept through her body. "I…" She wasn't used to talking to her lover like this, let alone having a man talk to her in such a sensuous way. That was a sad commentary on her love life.

Jared began tracing circles around her knee. "Tell me."

"I'm excited, but…" She took a deep breath. "I'm also scared."

"Yellow." His hand disappeared.

Angie glanced at him, and his expression was stone cold sober. "I didn't realize safe words went both ways."

"They do." He inhaled. "Are you scared of me?"

Her heart jumped. "No!" Without thinking she reached over and grabbed his hand from where it rested on his abs. "I'm not scared of you." How could she explain it?

Jared turned his hand over and entwined his fingers with hers. His gesture gave her strength. "I've never felt this way before, and it frightens me."

"I want you to tell me how you feel. Don't hide it from me."

"You sound like a psychologist."

He winced. "I'm a licensed sexual psychologist."

"A sex therapist?" Why did that surprise her? This man oozed sex and sensuality, plus he questioned her like a shrink.

"I don't counsel couples on their sex life, unless they specifically ask for it as part of their time on the ranch." He squeezed her hand. "The ranch exists for couples to discover their sexual selves in a place where no one is going to think them odd, unusual, or depraved."

A sliver of hope slipped under her skin. "You won't think I'm depraved, no matter what I say?"

"Nothing you say or do will make me think of you in any way other than as a woman I'm attracted to, a woman with sensual needs, and I will fulfill those needs, if I can. I do have my limits."

Angie tilted her head. She never thought about Dominants having limits before. This was so intriguing and so different than what she thought it would be.

She gave Jared a sly smile. "I'm waiting."

"For what?" His tilted his head in puzzlement.

"The right word."

He grinned. "Green."

"One of my favorite fantasies is pretty complicated."

"I want every last detail."

She took a breath. "I've come home from work. It's been a long day. I undress and head for the shower. My lover follows me and pushes me up against the wall and pins my hands behind my back with his body.

"'Be a good girl,' he tells me."

She shifted. "He guides me to the bed. My body is shaking. What is he planning?"

" 'Do I have your consent, my darling?' he asks me, and I tell him yes." Angie told him how her lover tied her up and used toys on her, then fucked her several times. Then he flipped her onto her stomach and spanked her. When he was done, they cuddled for a while.

"That's some fantasy." His gaze swept over her body. "Are you wet from telling me?"

"Yes." She closed her eyes.

"Let's see how wet." Before she could even form a word, he reached over, and his fingers delved into her pussy.

She moaned at his touch.

"Wet and needy." His words were soft. "But not just yet." He withdrew his hand.

She opened her eyes. "Not fair." How could he touch her like that, then leave her wanting more?

"Who said I played fair? Next fantasy, please."

Angie wanted to slap him. Instead, she took a deep breath. *I'll get even with him*, she vowed before she launched into her next fantasy.

***

Jared was having a hard time keeping his control. Every one of her fantasies revolved around her being submissive in sexual situations. Not surprising, since he had her pegged as a submissive the first time he met her.

The detail of her fantasies was amazing. She'd really thought about this, maybe even yearned for them to come true. He was going to enjoy fulfilling them for her. Whatever men she'd had in her life were total asses for not realizing what a gem they had. It had been a long time since he'd been this excited to be with a woman.

He had a feeling that Angie would tax him to the limit of his control, but *oh*, what fun they would have. His stomach growled. *Oh damn*. He glanced at his watch. He'd been so wrapped up in her fantasy and then his, he'd lost track of time. Hers had been extremely detailed, whereas he'd kept his shorter.

Angie was squirming, and he was sure she was so aroused that one touch to her clit and she'd shoot off like a Fourth of July rocket. This was what he wanted. To show her who was in control. She finished talking.

"Very good."

"What?" She blinked at him. "That's it?"

"For now. It's almost dinner time. After we eat, I'll show you the room we'll be spending most of our time in." A breeze brushed over his skin, reminding him they were outside.

"You're thinking about food?" Disbelief was written all over her face.

"My stomach is." It was a good thing he could keep his features neutral. His cock was raging, but he would maintain control. "Besides, we both need to keep our strength up." He ran his finger over her red cheek. "And you need to cool down."

"I don't want to cool down." She nipped at his finger, and he almost laughed.

"Too bad." He stood and then held a hand out to her. He'd have to remember to hose down the lounger.

She puffed out a breath, then put her hand in his. He pulled her to her feet and then picked up her skirt. "You can put your skirt back on or not. It's up to you."

Her body flushed as she snatched the fabric from his hand and slipped it back on. There was something to be said about skirts with elastic waistbands. "Would you like chicken or beef for dinner?" Jared asked as he held open the back door.

***

Angie squirmed as Jared placed the food on the table. "Dig in," he said after he took his seat. They both filled their plates.

Angie didn't feel like talking. She wanted to rail at Jared for leaving her so frustrated, but she had a feeling her ire would be met with amusement.

The only good thing was she saw the bulge of his cock pushing against the fabric of his jeans before he sat down, and that made her feel better that she wasn't alone in her frustration. He wanted her as much as she wanted him.

"I'm glad you're eating since you didn't eat a lot of lunch," Jared said.

"My appetite came back." She finished the last morsel on her plate.

"Good." He stood and cleared the table.

Angie stood and waited by the table, unsure what to do. He returned, took her hand, and guided her to the third floor.

"We're going to the bedroom where I'm staying?"

"No." He turned left instead of right toward her room. "This floor used to be Tyler's living space. When he and Becca moved to their own cabin, I redesigned it." He pulled a key out of his pocket, unlocked the door at the end of the hall, and pushed it open. With a sweeping motion of his hand, he announced, "Here's where we will spend a lot of our time."

Angie stepped into the room, and he followed. The walls had been painted a soft gray, not too dark, but not too bright. A very large, free-standing bed dominated one wall. Another wall held a set of cabinets, six in total.

Equipment sat neatly lined up against another wall. She could identify a spanking bench, but she had no clue about the other items. There were rings mounted to the walls and ceiling. A tremor ran up her spine just thinking about how Jared could use those rings with her. Then she spied a swing in the corner of the room.

Jared's heat surrounded her before his hands closed over her hips. "This is my special playroom." His breath brushed against her skin.

Angie was speechless. *Is this a real BDSM dungeon?* After she learned from Becca what the ranch was about, she'd seen pictures on various websites. But they didn't prepare her for the real thing.

"In the bed, I can restrain you in any way I want."

"But there's no headboard."

"Look closely at the bed." Angie stared at the bed. "Do you see them? There are under-mattress restraints hanging down."

"Clever." It was, and she wondered what else he had hidden in the room.

He pointed out each item as he continued. "There is a small kneeler I can use for punishments, but a spanking bench for other things."

Shivers chased each other through her veins. This room was straight out of her fantasies, and he said he'd redesigned the floor. *How long had he been planning to bring a woman to this room?* Her heart pounded.

"The chair in the back we'll talk about later."

Angie's gaze focused on the chair. It looked like any other wooden chair.

"Depending on my mood, I may restrain you to the wall or the hard points in the ceiling. Plus, I do have a swing." His lips touched her ear. "I can put you in that, and we'll have so much fun as I push you, and you impale yourself on my cock."

"And the cabinets?" His words were turning her on more than she thought possible. Maybe because he didn't hold back.

"Let's explore them. I want you to see what I have in store for you and make sure I don't violate any limits you might have." He released her waist.

With her knees shaking, Angie forced herself to walk over to the first cabinet. She kept her hands at her sides, not because she was afraid to open it, but she was waiting for Jared to give her permission.

"Open it," he said, standing behind her once again.

Praying her hands didn't tremble, she slid open the doors and gasped. There were rows of drawers and each was labeled. Vibrators, dildos, bullets and eggs, wands, and G-spot.

"Toy cabinet." He pulled open the drawers.

"So I see." Her pussy clenched. So much to explore. "I haven't seen this many since I went to an adult store."

"When did you visit this adult store?"

"A couple of years ago. I took Becca to get her first vibrator."

"Then why so surprised?"

"In an adult store, I expect a variety, but…" She waved her hand at the drawers and the rest of the cabinets. "I've never seen anything like this in a private home."

"I like to use any toy I want on my lover, as long as she doesn't mind." He closed all the but the dildo drawers. "I want my lover to be satisfied."

Angie's breath hiccupped. There were dildos from the size of her pinky finger all the way up to… A huge monster at the end. *How had his other lovers reacted to this?* She pushed the thought away, mainly because he said he'd only done this since Tyler moved out, and that was six months ago.

Jared pushed the drawer closed. "Go to the next cabinet and open it."

She obeyed him. These drawers were labeled: body lotions, body jewelry, blindfolds, anal, cock rings. She glanced up at Jared when she got to the cock rings.

"These will enhance our play, especially when I show you the right way to use them. Keep going."

One by one, Angie opened the cabinets. By the last one, she was a little bit in awe of what Jared had accumulated. Restraints, rope, handcuffs, floggers, paddles, canes, spreader bars, violet wand, and gags.

There were some items she never wanted to use, but others intrigued her. There was no way they could explore everything in two weeks, but the possibilities were there. "How many of these are we going to use?"

"As many as you want to try." His arms encircled her waist and pulled her against him. His hard cock pressed into her ass, and she barely prevented herself from rubbing against his erection.

"Are you wet?" he whispered.

"Yes."

"Good." He stepped back.

Her gut tightened. He was going to leave her hanging again.

"Tomorrow, you will be in this room at twelve-thirty. There will be an outfit waiting for you on the bed. Put it on and wait for me. I will be here at one sharp. At that time, we will begin by discussing limits and consequences for things like disobedience and topping from the bottom."

She shivered at the word punished. "What if I decide to leave in the morning?" Why did she say that? She had no intention of leaving. Exploring her sexual side with Jared would be safe. Wouldn't it?

"Your last chance." He turned her in his arms and cupped her chin and raised her face to his. "If you're here tomorrow afternoon, we will have the discussion I promised and explore and enjoy the things we will have learned about each other. On the other hand, if you are not here and dressed as instructed, this will be over and done, and we will never know what could have been. Do you understand?"

"Yes."

"Good." He brushed a kiss over her lips and nibbled his way to her ear. "Be prepared if you stay, because I'm going to tease, arouse, seduce, and fuck you until you scream. Then I'll do it over and over again." He released her.

All Angie could do was stare at his retreating back as he left the room. Her shoulders dropped, her breathing was short and choppy, and the abandonment feeling filled her. Jared had done it again: aroused her to the point of needing to be satisfied and left her hanging.

Well, he did say he was going to tease her. He was doing a damn good job of it. Her pussy clenched with need, and her skin was sensitive. She should be able to fix her arousal. She went to the first cabinet and opened the vibrator door.

Which one? There were so many. She ran her finger over the selections.

"No masturbation."

Angie spun around to see Jared lounging against the door jamb, grinning. He was back; he hadn't left her. Her spirits lifted. Then his words filtered into her brain. "What do you mean no masturbation?" He couldn't mean that.

"Just what I said. Close the drawer and come out of the room. I'll lock the door so you aren't tempted."

She huffed, closed the drawer, and marched over to him. He gestured for her to leave the room. That meant brushing by his hard body. *Two can play at this game.* As she passed him, her fingers grazed over his chest, lingering on his nipples. Once she was in the hall, he shut the door and locked it.

"You know I don't have to have a vibrator to masturbate."

"But you won't." His hands cupped her shoulders. "Anticipation. Think how sweet it will be tomorrow if you're sexually unfulfilled today."

"I guess you won't be taking your pleasure either." She lightly stroked his impressive bulge.

"I won't." He grasped her questing fingers and kissed each digit. "Oh, and I forgot to tell you. When I had your things moved, I kidnapped your battery-operated boyfriend." He dropped her hand and left.

"Bastard," she whispered, but she smiled. Jared was going to be a hard case to figure out, but she would. She liked puzzles.

Now to survive until tomorrow.

Chapter Four

♥

The next day, Jared worked through the morning without a break, anticipating his afternoon with Angie. She hadn't been happy with him leaving her without satisfaction, but he wanted her on edge. He wanted Angie to learn she couldn't manipulate him any way she wanted, because he suspected she was used to easily dominating men.

He wasn't one she could do that to. Never before had a woman stimulated him both physically and mentally. And he liked it. Jared went up the stairs to the third floor and into his special room. It was empty.

Disappointment hit him hard in the stomach. It wasn't the first time a woman couldn't handle his needs, but he'd had high hopes that Angie was different. She'd been so aroused yesterday. He hadn't read her wrong, he was sure of it.

Her increased breathing, flushing of the skin, the flash of desire and need in her eyes. He shook his head. It seemed in the cold light of day she couldn't handle him. He made his way across the room to close up the cabinets when she came flying into the room. She skidded to a stop when she saw him.

He took in the rumpled T-shirt, the messy hair, along with a pair of shorts and flip-flops. "You're late." He kept his tone level, even cold, but his heart unclenched with relief.

"I know. I'm sorry. I didn't fall asleep until early this morning and woke up five minutes ago."

Jared frowned. "Have you eaten?"

She shook her head.

"Let's go." He took her by the arm and led her downstairs to the kitchen. "Sit." Jared gestured to the small table and opened the fridge. He quickly assembled a sandwich for her, along with some cheese and fruit. "Eat."

She picked up the turkey sandwich and took a bite, then another one. Within a few minutes, the sandwich was gone, and she started in on the cheese and fruit. Jared grabbed a bottle of water and twisted the cap loose before he sat it in front of her.

Angie took a long drink, then polished off her food. Jared picked up the empty plate and set it in the sink; he could deal with it later. "Bring your water." He gestured for her to proceed him. Once back on the third floor, she stood in the middle of the room, staring at him.

"What time did you fall asleep?" he asked.

"Around five this morning."

"Why?"

"Why what?" She placed her water bottle on the small table and wrapped her arms around herself.

"What caused you to fall asleep so late?"

"Are you kidding me?"

The outrage in her voice almost made him smile. "Tell me, Angie."

"I was frustrated, okay? You left me hanging, yet again, and there was nothing I could do about it."

"You didn't masturbate?"

"You told me not to."

He grinned. "Good girl." She'd obeyed him. He wouldn't have blamed her if she had masturbated. Jared softened his tone. "Your outfit is on the bed; please put it on."

She walked to the bed and picked up the teddy he'd laid out for her. Her gasp filled the room. "Umm, isn't there something missing?" Her fingers tightened around the fabric.

"No." The teddy was crotchless and had cutouts where her breasts would be. It gave him full access to her body. She'd look fantastic in it. "You have two minutes to change."

"Where's the bathroom?"

"Here, behind the panel." He pushed against the panel and it popped open.

"Oh." She walked toward the door.

"Where are you going?"

"To the bathroom to change."

"You can change right here."

Jared folded his arms over his chest. "I'm soon going to see you without clothes anyway." He leaned against one of the cabinets, staring at her.

"Fine." She turned her back to him. Interesting. He'd already seen her naked pussy, but he wouldn't push her right at this moment

"Remove everything, I only want you dressed in the teddy," he mentioned when she still had her bra and panties on.

Angie said something under her breath that he didn't catch, but she kicked off her flip-flops, pushed down her panties, and he was greeted with the view of her ass. His blood heated. How would those pale globes feel when he spanked them? Paddled them? Flogged them?

His cock jerked as he watched her remove her bra and shimmy into the teddy. She then took her clothes and put them on a chair before turning to face him. The air left his lungs. He'd been sure the outfit would look great on her, but...

Shit.

The black lace cutouts hugged her full breasts, and the underwire lifted them to display them to their best advantage. Her hips shifted and he could see her pubic hair. He made a mental note to ask her about shaving another day. He didn't want anything hiding her charms from him.

"Turn around, please."

She glared at him but complied. Her ass was well displayed, the black G-string of the teddy dipping between her ass cheeks. His gaze roamed over her lace-covered back to where her hair covered the fastening around her neck. That would need to be fixed. He loved her lush hair, but it would only get in the way.

Pushing away from the cabinet, Jared crossed over to the table where her water sat and opened the drawer. He grabbed the hairbrush and ties he'd put in there yesterday, then moved the straight back chair from the corner and placed it in front of him.

"Come sit down."

Angie didn't say a word. Once she was seated, he gathered her hair in his hand. "You have beautiful hair." Her drew the brush through her tresses.

"Thank you."

"As much as I'd like you to keep it down, please braid it before you arrive each day." He separated her hair and began braiding it. Within minutes, he was done, and a sense of satisfaction flowed through him. He hadn't lost his touch.

"I've never had a man brush my hair before, let alone braid it."

"I'm glad I was your first. Please stand up, face the chair, bend over, and place your hands on the seat."

She hesitated for a moment before following his instructions. Jared put the brush away and then walked around Angie. He noted her rapid breathing and the slight shifting of her hips. Her nipples were taut, and her ass called to him.

"You were late today, and for being late, you will be punished." He brought his hand down on her ass.

"Ouch!" She straightened, her hands covering her ass.

Jared gently took her hands. "Today, I will be forgiving because this is your first day. From now on, you will hold your position until I tell you to move. Understand?"

"Yes." Her voice wobbled.

"I surprised you with the swat." He released her wrists and skimmed his palms over her arms. "Go lie faceup on the bed."

He probably should continue the punishment, but for some reason, he didn't want to. While Angie settled herself on the mattress, he stripped off his shirt. The fabric was beginning to irritate his skin. He was already barefoot, but he'd bet Angie hadn't noticed. "Arms over your head and spread your legs."

Once again, she hesitated before obeying him. "If your arms start to hurt or go numb, tell me."

She nodded.

"How are you feeling?"

"Vulnerable." Her voice sounded soft.

"That's understandable. What else is going on?" He moved around the bed, his gaze never leaving her. How the hell was he going to keep his control with her sexy body spread out before him?

"Confused."

It took him a second to realize she was answering his question. "Why confused?" He wanted her to talk to him, so he'd keep prompting her until she did it naturally.

"My mind is fighting against this, but my body is enjoying it."

He nodded. "Most people don't realize it, but the mind is a sexual organ as well. While many think the mind reacts more to visual stimuli, it's also emotions and sensations. When I swatted your ass, what were you thinking?"

"At first, I was outraged, but then heat spread through my body." Her lashes fluttered closed, and she curled her fingers into her palms.

"Makes sense." He could see her fighting to understand her feelings. "Forget what you were taught before, that sex and sexual stimulation are wrong. There's nothing wrong with being excited by a love tap, by a lover's touch, or how your lover looks at you." His gaze devoured her as he moved around the bed.

Her nipples grew harder. She wiggled on the mattress.

"Be still."

"I can't."

He stifled a grin.

***

How the hell could he expect her to keep still when he was looking at her with such longing. Like she was the most beautiful thing in the world. Anticipation filled her.

"You can be still, or I'll restrain you."

"You wouldn't." Why did she say that? She knew darn well he would. This man wasn't one she could wrap around her finger and that excited her.

"Your choice."

Damn Dominant. She forced her body to remain still and focused her gaze on the ceiling. Maybe if she didn't look at him, her body would settle down.

"You make me so hot," he said. "Your nipples are hard little pebbles. I can't wait to suck them and put clamps on them."

Damn! Heat swept through her, and her gaze sought him out.

"Your abs are quivering." He paused at the end of the bed and stared at her. "Your pussy is wet; I can see it."

Angie groaned and closed her eyes, fighting not to close her legs or shift on the bed.

"I should rub a special lotion on those perky nipples." She heard the *pop* of a bottle top. Cold lotion touched her nipple. "Enjoy my touch?" His fingers circled her nipples, rubbing the lotion on and around them. "I said special lotion, because soon, the blood will rush to your tits, and you'll fight to stay still as heat fills you before I nip, lick, and suck those rosebuds."

Oh God. Her heart almost stopped as he closed his mouth over her right breast. He was right; heat filled her, almost like someone had lit a fire. He lifted his head and did the same to her left breast. When he was done, she was practically panting.

"Now let's see how you react when I massage this onto your labia and clit. I suspect you won't be able to hold still." His fingers trailed down her body, then to her mound.

She moaned as he massaged her labia and clit. Her pussy clenched. She was so hot, and she wanted more from him. Needed more from him. Now.

"Tell me when it begins to be too much."

Goosebumps spread over her body as much as warmth surrounded her pussy. Her clit throbbed.

"Oh baby, your clit is so hard, begging for attention. I have a feeling if I touch it, you'll rock straight to a climax."

Oh God, yes, touch it. Her fingers clenched and un-clenched as she fought not to rock her hips into his touch.

"Instead, I'll slip a finger into your pulsing pussy."

She frowned. His fingers were still at her waist.

"Lord, you're clenching around my finger, trying to suck it into your depths."

How was this possible? He never moved his hands from her waist, but his words took her closer and closer to the edge.

Air blew across her sensitive breasts and then her clit. Her hips rose. "Oh God. Jared. Please."

"You do please me." He blew on her clit once again, and her pussy clenched.

She was unable to stop herself from shifting on the mattress. More, she needed more.

"So sensitive, so alive." His words brushed over her skin. "I'm going to slip another finger into your pussy, then a third. You take them. I'm stretching you so you can take me."

His words didn't match his actions, but her body reacted as if he was doing exactly what he described. "Touch me. Oh, please touch me." She was begging, and she didn't care. Her legs opened wider in an invitation.

"You're dripping. Lord, you can barely hold still as I pump my fingers in and out of you, your hips bucking in time with the motion. My mouth covers one nipple as I continue to fuck you with my fingers. And…"

Angie held her breath. She was so close.

"I'll place my thumb on your clit and rotate it hard and fast."

Air blew against her pussy and then her clit in quick bursts. Her stomach clenched, and her toes tingled. He wasn't even touching her, and she was ready to climax.

"That's it, baby, come for me. Let yourself go. Give it to me." The air was hotter against her skin. "Feel my fingers fucking you; your clit bursting. Your body wants this. Let it go. Move your body with my thrusts."

Her body undulated against the mattress. Images played behind her closed eyes. His fingers thrusting in and out of her pussy, his thumb on her clit, his lips on her nipples. She loved every second of this.

"Your clit is burning hot, throbbing beneath my thumb."

"Yes...fuck me. Make me come." Her hips rose, reaching for him.

"That's it. Let it overtake you. Show me your pleasure."

"I'm..." She cried out as he blew on her overheated clit, and her climax rolled through her. Tremors shook her body. She'd never felt anything like it.

"So very beautiful." His voice sounded far away.

Her body settled back against the mattress, and she forced her eyes open to see him standing next to the bed with his gaze on her face.

Wait a second? She shook her head. He'd touched her, hadn't he? He'd made her climax. His touch had been too real, hell, it was real. Her body still shook with aftershocks.

Jared knelt on the bed. "Perfect," he said before his lips captured hers.

She opened her mouth to him and didn't wait for him to take control. Her tongue thrust into his mouth, tangling with his, wanting his passion. Wanting more than just his voice. She wanted him.

Her tongue chased his, and her lips clung to his as he broke the kiss. "The mind is a beautiful thing." He brushed a kiss over her forehead. "Can you lower your arms?"

"I think so." She wiggled her fingers, then lowered her arms to her sides. Jared had already straightened.

"You did very well today, but then, I imagined you would. Your mind bought into the fantasy and that was wonderful."

"What?" She shook her head, trying to clear away the sensual haze. "You're ending our session now?" She couldn't believe it. Her body was on fire, and while she'd just climaxed, she wanted him in her.

"We've been at this for over an hour now."

"An hour?" How had so much time passed? "Please, you can't leave me like this."

"Like what, Angie?"

"Hot, wanting. I need your cock in me."

"And you will have it."

She smiled.

"When I'm ready to give it you and not before. Today was about listening to your body and letting your mind enjoy words and sensations. Dinner will be at five." He started for the door.

"Don't you dare leave me." He couldn't leave her abandoned. Not now. Not again.

Jared turned, and the impact of his stare caused her to suck in a breath. "Don't forget who is in charge here. Keep it up, and I'll paddle your ass until you can't sit down."

She drew her lip between her teeth. "I apologize, but Jared, how can you do this to me?"

"I've engaged your mind and body together. And don't forget, you've climaxed." He left the room with a wave.

Angie groaned as a tremor went through her body. He was right; she'd orgasmed without him even touching her. But he left her needing him. What kind of woman was she to allow that to happen? Her frustration level built along with her embarrassment.

Logically, she knew there was no reason to be embarrassed. He wanted her, yet for him, the more important issue was her climax, and he'd made it happen without even touching her. Not the way she wanted, but according to his plans. She should feel coveted, but the only thing her brain remembered was her wanting and him walking out the door. The not-so-wanton woman inside her cringed at her actions, and the abandoned side warned her Jared would never stay.

Chapter Five

♥

Jared whistled while he tossed the salad. He hadn't been at peace like this in a very long time. He stood at the counter, enjoying the warmth from the oven where their dinner cooked. This was all because of Angie.

His cock tightened. She was so responsive to him, so alive and so fuckable. He couldn't wait until he could sink his dick into her pussy. Lord, even his vocabulary was a little more graphic with her.

In their session today, she'd been so willing to obey him that he'd barely held on to his control. Yes, there were times where she wanted to defy him—he could see it in her body—but her submissive side proved stronger.

And how she didn't even realize what was happening to her pleased him more than he'd imagined. He was able to make her climax with words and the lightest of touches. That hadn't happened with other women before.

The timer on the oven dinged. He pulled the food out and put it on a hot pad before he carried it to the table along with the salad bowl. Angie was sitting at the table already, wearing what looked like a sundress, but he could see the outline of the black teddy underneath. He was surprised she was still wearing it.

Jared served up the salad and main dish, then paused. Tension thickened the air with her silence. He stared at her as he took his seat. Her body was stiff, too controlled, and her hands lay in her lap where he couldn't see them.

"Are you feeling okay?" he asked.

"Yes and no." She captured her lip between her teeth, and he forced himself to stay in his seat and not kiss her silly.

"What's bothering you?" He poured her a glass of wine.

She was silent until he set the bottle down and stared at her.

"You made me climax with only your words."

"Yes." He had a feeling there was more than she was saying, but this was their first day, and it wasn't the time to peel back the deeper layers. He'd ferret out what she wasn't saying later.

"That's never happened before." Her cheeks were pink.

"Your mind has never been engaged in sex." He cradled his chin in his palm. "You can tell me if I'm wrong, but with all your other lovers, you initiated the sex, right? You controlled every aspect of sex."

She nodded.

"Today, I controlled it. All I did was engage your mind in the sexual act."

"You did more than that." A flush pinkened her skin. "All I can think about is how fantastic I felt today."

"Good. That's how it should be."

"No, it's not." She shifted in her chair. "I don't like being constantly aroused."

"Liar."

Her mouth dropped open, and he fought against grinning. She didn't have a clue her body was made for this, her mind as well. He'd show her over and over again.

"I don't lie."

"Really." Jared stood and moved around the table to stand behind her chair. He gently cupped her shoulders. "You're lying to yourself." Touching her was becoming a habit, but it was one he enjoyed. "Shall I raise your dress and prove how wet you are?"

Her body trembled with her intake of breath.

"Because I know you're wet. Your tits are heavy, and your nipples are poking out. The fact that you're still wearing the teddy is telling."

Her head dropped.

Jared knelt next to her, cupped her chin and turned her face to his. "It tells me that you're a responsive, sexual woman who wants to please me, and there's not a damn thing wrong with that. I'm enjoying how you react to me." He took her lips in a brief, hard kiss before he stood and took his seat. "Now, let's eat."

"Such manners." Laughter tinged her voice.

Good. Her mood grew lighter. More than anything, Jared wanted his sub happy. *My sub?* Where had that come from? Giving himself a mental shake, he tucked the thought away for another time. "My mom would paddle my ass if she heard me talking like this at the dinner table. Of course, I wouldn't do it if she was here."

Angie's fork paused on the way to her mouth. "How does your mother feel about you running an adult ranch?"

His gut tightened. "I don't know. She died when I was eighteen."

"I'm sorry."

"Thank you." He swallowed. "I miss her. She was my rock. She was also the one who told me to be me and never apologize for it." He never would. Any woman he had a relationship with knew what he expected, especially his preference for a lot of sex and kinky sex. If they couldn't handle that, then he bid them good-bye. Life on his terms.

Sticking to one-night stands at a club he knew had always been enough for him. This two weeks with Angie would be good for him, though. It wouldn't be a lasting relationship. No woman wanted his sexual preferences for a lifetime.

"She was a smart woman."

"Yes." He pushed away his thoughts about his mother. "You and Becca have a close relationship. Have you known her since childhood?"

"No." Angie stopped eating. "I was abandoned as a kid, put in foster care, and eventually I was adopted."

"That's rough." His heart went out to her. Navigating the foster care system wasn't easy, especially for a child. Her features were stoic, as if she'd put up an emotional wall around this topic. He was pleased she shared that with him. It also gave him insight into her need for control. Was this what made her pause earlier? Only time would answer that.

"I survived." She resumed eating.

Jared followed suit. He was interested in her life and wanted to know more. But he didn't have the right to question her unless he was willing to share more about his life, which he wasn't. Being with Angie was about sex and their reactions to each other. It couldn't be anything else. He wouldn't allow it.

After they finished, she helped him clear the table and load the dishwasher. He took her hand as they walked up the stairs to her bedroom.

"Tomorrow, at one, in the room. Please wear the same outfit. Since the material is delicate, please wash it in the sink, if you want, and it will be dry by morning." He leaned down and brushed a light kiss over her lips. "I have a meeting in the morning and then have some paperwork to do. The kitchen is fully stocked, so help yourself to whatever appeals to you. Be sure you eat something. You'll need the energy. See you at one."

He gave her another kiss before he turned and left her alone. His cock protested every step he took away from her. Jared figured he might as well get a jump start on the paperwork, since sleep wasn't going to come easy for him tonight.

***

The next afternoon, Angie stood by the bed in the playroom, staring out the window. The sunflowers were blooming, their faces raised toward the shining sun. A metaphor if she ever saw one. She felt like she was opening up to her sensuality.

"Please go lie on the bed."

She jumped at Jared's commanding voice. Taking a deep breath, Angie did as he commanded and laid down. The rustling of clothes caused her to turn her head to see Jared stripping off his pants.

Angie gasped. He was hard. Very hard.

Unable to help herself, she licked her lips and wondered how he would taste. Hopefully, she'd find out soon enough.

"Arms over your head and spread your legs."

Angie complied and jumped when his hand came into view.

"Relax, sweetheart," he said, touching her forehead. "Today, I want you to talk to me as I play with you. Close your eyes and tell me everything you're feeling."

The tips of his fingers feathered over her eyelids, barely disturbing her lashes. "Your touch is soft." Her voice was nearly a whisper.

He smoothed his fingers over her cheeks, to her ears, to her chin, and down her neck.

She lifted her shoulders. "Tickles." Angie opened her eyes and found Jared staring at her.

He skimmed over her collarbone, traced the sides of her breasts to her belly button, until he finally touched her hips and legs.

"You're wet."

"I'm always wet when I'm around you." She wanted to recall her words. *I've never been this open with a lover, but with Jared, things are different.*

He circled around the bed twice, silently, and Angie squirmed.

"Be still."

"Touch me."

"What?" he snapped.

"Please, touch me." *I need to feel his skin against mine.*

He tapped his chin, then opened the drawer of the nightstand and pulled out a blindfold. "I want you to use your other senses." He slipped the blindfold over her eyes.

Angie shivered. The loss of her sight made her a little nervous. Taking a deep breath, she concentrated on her hearing. At first, she couldn't hear anything but her rapid breathing, but as she adjusted, she realized she'd heard a slight noise.

She wasn't sure what it was. Then Jared's heat caressed her skin. He was close to her. A ripple of excitement rushed through her body. Something soft brushed over her right nipple. It was light, and it tickled.

He swirled it.

"*Ahh.*" Her back arched, and her grasped his shoulder.

"Bad girl," he whispered, his breath cool against her heated skin.

Jared's fingers encircled her wrist, lifted her arm over her head, and then he captured and lifted her other arm. Soft fabric encircled her wrists.

Whatever Jared used to tie her up with was silky. Scarves maybe. She jerked her arms. There was a little give in the restraint, but not so much she could slip free. A shaft of anticipation ran up her spine. Was he making one of her fantasies come true?

"Since you can't keep your hands to yourself," he said, "I've decided to help you."

Her body bucked when whatever he held in his hand touched her nipple once again.

"Can't you be still?"

"What is that?" She didn't want him to stop, but she couldn't help squirming. Angie bit her lip. If she was honest with herself, she enjoyed his teasing. A lot.

"You tell me."

Damn man. She tried to concentrate, but he moved the item over her stomach to the top of her thighs. Instinctively, she closed her legs.

"Open up."

She shook her head.

"Open." His voice was firm.

"No, Jared." She didn't think she could take it if he used whatever he was teasing her with on her pussy. Maybe she should use her safe word? But he wasn't hurting her, and her body tingled with excitement.

"I expect you to obey me." Before she could answer him, he seized her right ankle.

"Jared." Her breathing increased. Lord, how could she be turned on by this?

"I'm here, sweetheart." His touch was gentle as he restrained her legs. "Such a pretty pussy." The toy, or whatever it was, brushed over her pussy. The tickling sensation vibrated through her body. "Tell me what I'm using on you."

Angie forced herself to concentrate. "It's a feather."

"Yes. I'm using an ostrich feather tickler. It's made to tease your skin."

"It's doing its job." She squirmed as he swept it over her nipples once again. Damn, they were so sensitive. Then it was gone. Angie laid there panting and waiting. What was he going to do next?

The sound of a drawer opening and closing caused her to tense with anticipation, but nothing happened. After several deep breaths, her muscles started to relax. Jared's breath brushed her breasts right before his mouth closed over one nipple.

"Oh, yes." Angie breathed out.

He flicked it with his tongue before drawing it deep into his mouth. His tongue drew circles around the areola before zeroing in on the tip.

"Oh, God, that feels so good."

"Needy nipples." His breath brushed over her breasts as he spoke. "Let's see what I can do to make them satisfied."

Angie pondered his words. She felt Jared's fingers on her right breast, followed seconds later by a slight pinch, immediately followed by a pinch to her left nipple. A tremor shook her body. She was pretty sure he'd just put clamps on her nipples.

"I want you to see." He took the blindfold away and placed a pillow under her head. "You look beautiful in my clamps."

Angie blinked, then focused in on her breasts. Two metal clamps squeezed her nipples, and there was a chain trailing from them over her stomach. Her legs were spread wide. She was fully exposed to Jared and whatever he wanted to do. Her gut clenched.

Her body throbbed with everything that was happening to her, and it wasn't an unpleasant sensation. "It's different, but it feels good."

"I hoped it would." He blew air over her exposed breasts, and her body bucked. "So responsive. How about this?" He tugged the chain.

"That feels… I don't know. You're tugging my nipples. There's a bit of pain, but my pussy is pulsing."

Jared dropped the chain between her breasts, then removed a toy from the first cabinet and concealed it. "Close your eyes."

She bit her lip but did as he said. The second he touched her pussy, her eyes opened. He was staring at her.

"If you can't keep them closed, I'll put the blindfold back on."

"Yes, Sir." She scrunched her eyes shut. Her fingers curled into her palms when he touched her pussy.

"So pretty, so pink." He trailed his fingers through her wetness. "Aroused and ready."

"Yes." She lifted her hips.

"Not yet, sweetheart."

She moaned when his touch disappeared, only to groan when something cold and hard replaced them. A vibrator? Dildo? No, the shape wasn't right for those toys. Angie concentrated on the object. It was small, but wide. Jared's fingers were there, pushing deep into her pussy. Squirming against the mattress, she tried to figure out what the object was.

"You're wiggling again." He flicked one of the clamps, and she gasped. A shaft of pleasure shot from her nipple to her clit.

"I can't help it. You're teasing the hell out of me."

"Yes, I am." His breath brushed over her cheek before his lips found hers.

She opened her mouth to his, and their tongues tangled, tasting each other. He tasted so good, like mint and male. She devoured his lips, pulling at his tongue, wanting more, more of him. Angie tugged at the restraints on her wrists, wanting to touch him, to run her fingers through his hair, to feel the muscles of his back.

"*Mmmm.*" He smacked his lips. "I can't wait to see my dick between those sweet lips."

"Yes, please." Her words surprised her. She usually wasn't so eager to suck cock, but with Jared, what she usually wanted wasn't in the plan.

"Later. Have you figured out what I put in your pussy?"

"No. Someone keeps distracting me."

"I like distracting you."

The toy began vibrating, and her hips bucked. "It's not a bullet; it feels too big." She wrinkled her nose. "Oh, damn, it's one of those vibrating eggs."

"Very good." He brushed his lips over hers. "Do you know your clit is begging for attention?"

"I'm sure it is. Oh god..." He turned the egg vibration up, and her nerves pulsed, her pussy clinching around the egg.

"What shall I do with this eager clit?" His soft touch trailed over her stomach to the top of her mound, hovering above her clit.

"Touch me, please."

"Soon." He trailed his hands over her abdomen, over her ribs, until he reached her breasts. "Time to release the clamps." He leaned over her. "This might sting."

Angie's breath hissed out as he removed the clamp, but then his mouth was there, soothing away the pain. The second one was easier.

"What shall I do now?" He pressed the remote in his hand, and the egg vibration increased.

"Damn it." Her hips shifted.

"Do you know how beautiful you look? Your nipples are taut and rosy. Your pussy is gleaming, my egg is vibrating in you, and your clit is crying for attention."

Her breathing hitched at his words and her stomach tightened. His words increased her desire. If he would just touch her clit. "Please, Jared. Touch my clit."

"I think I will."

Relief poured through her. He'd get her off this precipice. But nothing happened. "Jared?"

"I'm right here, sweetheart."

By the sound of his voice, he was over by the cabinets. Angie was tempted to open her eyes to verify, but decided to let him surprise her. She drew in a sharp breath when he touched above her pussy, and something closed over her clit. It wasn't his mouth or his fingers.

"Ready to come?"

"Yes." She was past ready. Her body was primed.

The egg vibration increased, and something sucked at her clit. Her hips flexed, and she tugged at her hands and feet. "Jared, what have you done?" She'd never experienced anything like this. Exhilaration coursed through her body, but her release wouldn't come. The exhilaration kept climbing.

"Feel my toys: the egg deep in your pussy and the sucker on your clit."

The sucking became stronger. Oh Lord, it had to be only a matter of time before she exploded. Her toes tingled, then her belly. Angie opened her mouth, trying to get more air. Higher and higher, her body wound until, at last, her orgasm rolled through her.

When she could finally catch her breath, she realized Jared hadn't turned off his toys. If anything, they were turned up even higher.

"Please, Jared, stop."

"Come for me again. You're so beautiful when you come."

"I can't." Hell, coming once was amazing, but more than once? Her head thrashed against the mattress as her body stiffened when another climax rolled through her, and before it subsided, a third one hit.

Angie panted to get more air. Her body was on fire. She pulled at the restraints, but they held strong. She couldn't take any more.

"No more," she whispered.

"One more." His voice was soft, his breath brushing her ear. "You can do it."

His fingers were at her nipples, and he pinched them, hard.

Angie screamed as another orgasm slammed through her body. She couldn't handle it. Her body writhed on the bed until the vibrations and the sucker on her clit were turned off. Even then, her body twitched with the aftermath.

"So beautiful, so responsive, and so much mine." His lips grazed over hers. With gentle touches, he withdrew the toys and removed the restraints, then he massaged her arms and legs. "You did fantastic today."

Her lashes fluttered open, and she was surprised to see the room bathed in the soft light of early evening. "What time is it?" As badly as she wanted Jared inside her, she was glad they were done for today. Her body needed to recover.

"Almost six. Lie there and relax. I'll be right back."

Angie laid there and stared at his sexy ass as he sauntered from the room. She sighed and closed her eyes. Her bones were like jelly, but she wondered what was taking Jared so long. Her skin still tingled from her orgasms. Damn, she'd never imagined she could have multiple climaxes or that a man could do that to her.

She shifted. How long had Jared been gone? Angie turned onto her side and curled up, her body suddenly cold. His *right back* was longer than she expected. What would happen if he didn't return? Why did everyone abandon her? Was she a difficult person to get along with?

She didn't think so, but something in her was certainly lacking. Jared didn't stay. Maybe she'd call him on it later. Right now, she didn't want to move. Maybe if she curled into a little ball, these feelings would go away, and in a few hours, she'd find her strength.

***

Jared went to his room and straight into the shower. The cool water cascaded over his heated body. Angie was fantastic. Watching her orgasm over and over again had his cock hard and demanding attention.

But he wasn't in the mood to take care of it, right now. Shutting off the water, he dried off and dressed. He needed some air to think. He jogged down the stairs and out onto the back patio.

Fresh air and the scent of pine filled him as he took a deep breath and gathered his thoughts. He wanted to go back and be with Angie, but if he stayed with her, he'd bury his unruly dick in her pussy and never leave.

That didn't surprise him; he'd almost lost it while he played with Angie. The woman turned him on so much, he could barely control himself. Fucking her at this stage wouldn't be good. Mainly because he had so much to teach her yet, but also because he wasn't sure he was emotionally ready to lose himself in her.

With a shake of his head, he turned and headed back inside and to the playroom. Angie was curled on her side, sound asleep. He scooped her into his arms and carried her to her bedroom.

"You came back." Her voice was sleepy, but he noticed the tear streaks on her cheeks. Did she think he wasn't coming back? He'd ask her about it tomorrow.

"It's only been a few minutes." Gently, he placed her on her bed.

"Stay." Her arms reached for him.

"Okay." Normally, he'd do aftercare and leave, but they'd had a pretty heavy session. Plus, her tears. Jared climbed into the bed and nestled her against his body, then pulled the light blanket over them.

Angie snuggled close. "Thank you for not leaving. Everyone leaves."

Is that what the tears had been about? A fear of abandonment? Before he could ask her what she meant, she let out a small snore. He'd have to ask her about the "everyone leaves" remark. But for right now, he'd enjoy having her in his arms.

His emotions were all over the place. He was worried about Angie's tears. And about his own feelings. While they were at the beginning of their explorations, he was more than enamored with her.

Her moans of pleasure, the way her skin turned pink as he stroked it. Her cries of pleasure. She was a treasure in his eyes. A woman who could let go for him. Part of him wanted to retreat, and the other part wanted to bask in the enjoyment of Angie. He had to remember though, women didn't want a steady diet of kinky sex, and there was no reason for him to think Angie was different.

***

The next morning, Jared arranged the toys and other items he wanted on the table in the playroom. He was going to push Angie a bit further today. She'd given him everything she had to give yesterday. Angie had reveled in his sexual play. Jared rubbed his brow. He was sure she would tire of his type of play. Until then, though, he planned to enjoy every moment.

He'd fallen asleep with her last night, and they'd missed dinner because they'd both slept through the night. He remembered the feeling of her soft body against his, and still heard her soft sighs as she slept. Leaving her alone this morning had been one of the hardest things he'd ever done, something that surprised him.

But he'd done it. First, he'd fixed her breakfast and left it in the warming oven. Then he'd returned to her room with a note telling her the coffee was fresh and where to find her food.

He fought the desire to climb back into bed with her this morning. *Soon*, he promised himself. They had a lot more to explore. Now that he was finished with arranging the playroom, He spent the next hour in his office, torturing himself with boring but necessary paperwork. Once that was done, he rubbed his forehead as he walked out to check the progress of the renovations. The new cabins they were adding to the ranch already looked good, as did the renovations to the existing cabins. Excitement flowed through him.

"Morning, Jared. We're moving along at record pace," the foreman said.

"It looks great. I received confirmation that the material you need for the lecture rooms will be here tomorrow."

"Perfect. Would you like a tour of what we've done so far?"

"Later this week. I've some work take care of, but I wanted to see how things were going."

"Have fun with the paperwork. I hired my wife to handle mine. Best thing I ever did."

Jared chuckled, then walked away. *Maybe it was time to find another couple to work at the ranch and take some of the paperwork off his hands.*

***

Angie glanced at the clock. Five to one. *Damn.* She finished drying her hair and jogged out of her room. She couldn't be late. Jared would punish her if she was. Not that it bothered her, but she wanted to make him proud.

He'd come back to her last night and something inside her softened when he had. She was disappointed when she woke this morning and he was gone, but there was a note on his pillow, and her heart warmed. *Maybe staying here with Jared hadn't been such a bad idea after all.*

She skidded to a stop when she saw Jared waiting for her inside the playroom. "I'm not late."

"No, you're not." His eyes sparkled, and she wondered what he had in store for her today. Her heart pounded. Yesterday, he'd given her four orgasms. Something she hadn't expected.

"Please strip."

Angie swallowed. She'd worn the teddy again. Reaching up, she undid the snap behind her neck and let the fabric slide over her body to pool at her feet.

"On the bed."

"Ummm." She glanced at the bed, and there was a big black thing sitting there. It looked like a big wedge. Okay, how was she going to do this? Climbing onto the mattress, she stayed on her knees as she stared at the thing.

"On your stomach, please."

That made sense since the big end of the wedge was positioned where she would lay. Crawling over, Angie put her knees against the fabric and, using her arms, lowered herself over the wedge. Her ass was in the air, her upper body supported by the rest of the wedge. Vulnerability hit her hard in the gut.

The mattress dipped when Jared knelt on it. He massaged her back, and she relaxed. "I don't want to restrain you today, so keep your hands to yourself, and spread your legs."

"In this position, keeping my hands to myself won't be a problem." She shifted her knees apart. Her skin tingled with excitement.

"So true. If today works out the way I think it will, tomorrow we can have some real fun."

What was he planning? Her nerves danced with anticipation.

She heard a small *pop*. "Are you ready?"

"For what?"

"You mentioned you tried a butt plug before."

"Yes." She clenched her ass. He was going to play with her ass. Fear mingled with anticipation. She couldn't help tensing up.

"Easy." He rubbed her lower back. "Do you remember what size?"

"No. But I don't think it was very big."

"All right." Angie jumped as he ran his hands over her ass. "Easy, sweetheart. This is just lube." He ran his lubed-up fingers between her cheeks. "One of the major issues with ass play is not using enough lube." Liquid was poured over her ass. "It's important to use a lot. Pleasure, not pain, is the goal."

His tone was calm as he caressed her, and she began to relax. His finger slid to her anus. Her heart stopped.

"Easy," he whispered. His fingers probed, and one slipped in, spreading the lube around. "I'm adding a second finger now. I want you to breathe out."

She puffed out a breath as he pressed a second finger into her. Angie fought not to squirm. It didn't hurt, but she couldn't catch her breath. She heard him squeeze the bottle of lube, but nothing hit her skin.

"You're doing so well." He moved his fingers in and out of her ass. "Now, take another breath and push out."

Angie did as he asked; she felt his fingers slip out and something take their place. Something hard.

"Jared?" Her voice wobbled.

"It's okay, sweetheart." He paused for a moment before he rubbed her lower back in gentle circular motions. "How does it feel?"

"Different. When I tried one before, it hurt, and my ass continued to burn even after I took it out." This toy stretched her but didn't really hurt.

"Probably too big for you. Where did you get it?"

"An adult store. The guy told me I'd like it."

Jared chuckled. "Tip: Always shop when there is a female employee. Women know women's bodies. What about lube?"

"He said to use a little bit, but…" She gasped as he adjusted the toy.

"Ass. He probably jacked off thinking about you shoving that too-big plug up your ass." The mattress shifted. "Are you ready for more?"

"More what? Isn't one butt plug enough?"

"I'm not talking a butt plug, that will stay in for a bit. I'm talking other things Let me make sure you're wet enough." He trailed his fingers over her pussy.

Angie wiggled. His touch pushed her need up another notch, especially with the toy in her ass. This was so unexpected and yet, not.

"Your clit is swelling." He withdrew his fingers and then placed a toy at her entrance.

"What is it?" she asked out of curiosity.

"A thin vibrator." He traced her outer lips. "Half-inch wide and seven inches long."

Her mouth dropped open as he pushed it into her pussy. "Oh my goodness." The vibrator pushed against the plug in her ass. It wasn't unpleasant; it was different and made her body heat.

"Easy." With one hand he stroked her back in those same soft circles while he slid the vibrator in and out with the other. More than anything else, his concern for her well-being relaxed her.

Her focus changed as the two toys inside her made her body burn with need. "More," she whispered, surprising herself.

Jared didn't say anything. Instead, he continued to play with the vibrator until it was fully seated in her pussy. "God, I love seeing you filled with my toys." He twisted the plug in her ass again.

Angie squealed, but raised her ass up.

"That's it. Move with me."

She wasn't sure how much she could move, lying the way she was. Jared turned on the vibrator, and she moaned.

"How are you doing, baby?"

Angie tried to catch her breath. The pulses from the vibrator echoed in her ass, causing her to tighten around both toys. "I'm good." Any better and she'd probably be dead.

"That makes me happy." He continued to play with the plug in her ass as his other hand held the vibrator in her pussy.

Her climax built before she realized it. Her toes curled as the tingles swept through her body.

The vibrator was turned off.

"No!" she cried out.

"We've got a lot more to cover today."

He removed both toys. Angie sighed. He was going to tease her again today? Could she handle it? Yes, she could. She would, even if it killed her.

Jared played with her body for hours. He used nipple clamps, vibrators, bullets. He'd take her to the brink of climax and then stop until her body settled down. Angie decided his mouth should be registered as a weapon as he kissed, licked, and devoured every inch of her body.

Now his mouth was on her clit, his tongue teasing it. Her body was primed and ready. Was he going to stop this time? Her need grew higher and high until she was thrashing against the bed. She was almost there.

Jared plunged two fingers into her pussy, and she screamed. Her orgasm rolled over her. It continued even after Jared removed his fingers and stopped licking her. She laid there, deliciously satisfied.

"You are wonderful." His lips trailed over her belly. "How do you feel?"

"Satisfied."

"Good." He laid beside her and then cradled her body against his.

It was nice to be held like this. Very few of her lovers ever held her after sex. Most of the time, they did what she asked them to, then got up, disposed of the condom, dressed and left. It made her feel abandoned and alone. But Jared was still here.

She could get used to his cuddling and wondered if that was a good thing or not. And they hadn't even fucked yet.

She sighed. "What's on the agenda for tomorrow?" she asked.

His lips caressed her ear. "If I told you, it wouldn't be a surprise."

"Tease."

"You have no idea. Close your eyes and rest."

"Stay," she whispered before her eyes closed.

"I will."

***

Jared stared down at Angie's serene face. This woman turned him on so much. She was wiggling her way into his emotions even though he fought against it. They'd only been together three days, and she'd met every expectation. She amazed him.

She was more than willing to explore with him. He'd have to watch himself. He could easily fall in love with her, and that was not an option in his book. Admire her, lust after her, yes, but never love.

Would he ever find a woman out there who understood and enjoyed kink as much as he did. And that was what he wanted, a lifetime with a partner who enjoyed exploring sexual pleasure as much as he did.

He shifted but kept Angie close. Tomorrow, his raging cock would get some relief. Tomorrow, he would know just how far he could go with Angie. Anticipation built inside him. For the first time, that excitement was tinged with anxiety. Would she reject him, or would she be the woman he had begun to hope she could be?

A woman who accepted him for the person he was? A woman who would stay?

Chapter Six

♥

Angie stretched as she woke the next morning. She was a bit disappointed Jared wasn't in bed with her in her room. He'd mentioned he had an early meeting and didn't want to wake her. It still didn't stop the loneliness filling her.

Yawning, she climbed out of bed and went into the bathroom. A quick shower, breakfast, and she'd see if Jared was in his office. Sitting around in the mornings doing nothing was starting to get to her.

She turned to close the bathroom door and a hard male body slammed into hers. The air was knocked out of her lungs and her arms were pinned to her side. Angie kicked out and missed.

Shit. *Relax. Pretend to faint and he'll let you go.* She forced her muscles to go lax in his hold.

"Good try," a deep voice murmured against her ear as his hold tightened.

"Jared." She knew his voice. How had he snuck in here?

"Good guess." He tightened his arms around her. "Ready to act out your fantasy?"

She'd forgotten about that. "Please," she whispered.

"I'll please you all right." He forced her arms behind her and tied her wrists. Angie tried to squirm away but couldn't. Fabric was slipped over her eyes. She cried out.

"Easy, sweetheart. I have you." His breath fanned over her bare shoulder.

Why hadn't she slipped on a night shirt when she got up? She never walked around naked. This was all Jared's fault. He was getting her used to being without clothes in the bedroom. Not that he hadn't see it all before. Jared moved back, and she could feel the weight of his gaze on her body.

Another cry left her lips when he spun her around, and her feet left the ground as he lifted her onto his muscular shoulder. With her arms secure behind her back, she couldn't hit him. She tried thrashing her legs.

"Be still." He smacked her ass.

"Damn! That stung."

Concentrate. Where was he taking her? *Breathe. Slow and steady, don't let him get to you.* She heard his steps and realized he was headed down the hallway. Was he taking her downstairs?

No, he turned right, not left. The squeak of a door opening. That was the playroom. She remembered the door squeak from the other day. But why wasn't the door locked? It had been up until now. Jared must have unlocked it earlier.

She took a deep breath. Sandalwood and pine filled her senses. Her muscles relaxed as she was placed on the bed, on her stomach.

"Such a beautiful ass." His fingers danced over her skin.

She squirmed under his touch. No one else she'd been around smelled like he did. Straining, she tired to hear him, but nothing. *Wait.* A light scraping sound. Maybe furniture being moved?

Angie stiffened when she was picked up again. Cold leather touched her knees, and his hand was at her back, pushing her forward. Her chest lay against some sort of support. The bindings around her wrists loosened.

Before she could pull them away, he raised her arms over her head and bound them again. She struggled. Unable to see anything, she wasn't sure what he was doing.

She squirmed and shifted her knees, hoping she could get some leverage. His body pressed against hers and his hard cock nestled into the crack of her ass. She tried to buck him off.

"Stop struggling."

"Let me go." She had to remember this was her fantasy. A little bit of forced seduction with someone she trusted.

"Naw."

"Please?"

"I will please you, sweetheart."

Her breath rushed out of her. His use of the word sweetheart calmed her nerves. She pushed away her fear and concentrated on his touch. His fingers trailed along her spine.

"Such smooth skin." His breath brushed over her, and a shiver flowed through her body. "I'm going to have so much fun today. Let me tell you what I'll do. First, I want to warm this pretty little ass, then I'm dying to taste that sweet pussy of yours until you're begging me to let you come. Plus, I have some other surprises for you."

Angie bit her lip. She needed to play her part.

"Please, please don't hurt me." She pleaded, hoping it was enough.

"I'm not into giving nonconsensual pain." He cupped her ass. "Now to warm these globes." Jared lifted his hand.

She missed his touch. As long as he was touching her, she was safe. Who was she kidding? She was safe with

Jared. He would never hurt her physically. The sound of a cabinet opening caused her to tense up.

What was he grabbing?

Focus.

Forcing her muscles to relax against the bench, she waited. There was a slight swishing sound before something hit her right ass cheek.

"Ouch!" Her exclamation came more from surprise than pain. Her ass stung, but it faded within seconds.

Another swish and her left ass cheek was hit. Before she could draw in another breath, he struck her again.

Oh my goodness. Her pussy clenched with each strike. He wasn't hurting her; he was heating her up. Warmth spread from her ass and though her body with each blow. She finally realized he was using a flogger, one that made her hotter with each impact.

Soft fabric teased the small of her back before caressing the inside of her thighs. "I love a red ass."

"I bet you do." *Keep in character.* "Let me go now; you've had your fun."

"Not yet. I haven't tasted you. Are you wet yet?"

She played the outraged captive. "Of course not."

"Oh, I think you are. I'll see for myself." He swiped a finger over her pussy. "My little liar." The flogger caressed her ass. "What shall I do for you lying to me?"

"Nothing." She jerked at the restraints, not really trying to get away.

"I have to do something. Maybe one of my new toys."

New? Angie tried to remember what she'd seen in the cabinets but came up blank. Straining to hear anything, she waited. It seemed like hours before he spoke.

"This would have been better if I had restrained you faceup, but then I couldn't play with your ass like this." His hands caressed her ass, then slid between her spread legs. "I wonder how much hotter you can get." His fingers parted her pussy lips. A round object touched her pussy. It was warm as he coated it in her wetness. "That's it, sweetheart." Jared pressed it into her.

"What the hell is that?"

"It's a very special dildo." He maneuvered it in and out of her wet core.

She'd never experienced anything like this. Heat spread from her pussy to the rest of her body, but it was more than that. "Hot." Was the dildo getting hotter?

"This dildo was made to be heated up in hot water or cooled off in icy water."

Her mouth dropped open, and he pushed it farther into her. The dildo itself was smooth, almost like glass, and teased her nerve endings as he pulled it out and then pushed it back in.

"Oh yes, fuck me with it." *Damn, where had those words come from?* It was only because this was Jared.

"Not yet."

She cried out as he pulled the dildo from her.

"Let's try this one."

Another cry left her lips as he pushed the ice cold one into her. He thrust it a few times and then removed it. Angie was panting. Her body shivered, not only from the cold of the dildo, but the excitement running through her veins.

"Quit teasing me."

"That's all part of the fun." The mattress dipped as Jared climbed off.

Angie laid there, trying to catch her breath, wondering what he had in store for her next. This man was diabolical. The bed dipped, and she heard the flip of a top. Cool lube dribbled on her ass and down her crack. He slipped a finger into her ass.

"No. No. Please don't use my ass this way." She forced a note of begging into her voice. They were still role playing, even if she'd gotten out of character a bit.

He hesitated. "Sweetheart, are you okay?" His voice was soft. "Are you playing into the fantasy?" The concern in his voice was evident.

"I'll use my safe word if you go too far."

He swatted her ass. "I won't stop again unless I hear your safe word."

A second finger joined the first. "I love the way your ass grips my fingers. Your pussy is twitching. I can't wait until I can fuck your ass."

Angie stiffened and opened her mouth.

"But not today." He added more lube.

She blew out a breath.

"When I pull my fingers out, breathe in and then out." She did as he asked, and her breath whooshed out of her as he pushed a new toy in. "So beautiful," his voice was tender.

This toy was different. It wasn't the same butt plug he used yesterday; this one was small but seemed heavier.

"I love the look of your ass filled with my toys." He slipped two fingers into her pussy. "So wet and wanting. Let's see what I can do."

Angie tried to recall more of her fantasy but couldn't. Had she been vague with him, mainly being ravished by someone who was forcing her? Although he really hadn't had to force her once she figured out it was him.

A small, round toy was pushed into her pussy. *An egg?* It didn't feel round enough, and when he pushed it into her, she felt a tug on the one in her ass.

"What have you done?" she asked, gasping at the surge of heat that raced through her.

"Making sure you are fulfilled." He ran his hands over her inner thighs, then under her hips. "Up." He lifted her. With her being restrained, there wasn't much room, but somehow, he slipped fabric beneath her. Now, there was something against her clit. A strip of fabric was pulled over her pussy and ass. His fingers played with the other ends of the fabric at her back, then the material tightened.

"Ready, my sweetheart?"

"Ready for what?" What had he done?

"This." All three toys started vibrating.

"Shit." Her body stiffened.

"Easy." His hands massaged her back and shoulders. "This is for your enjoyment." The vibrations grew stronger.

Enjoyment? She tried to shift her hips without much success. Her nipples rubbed against the bench as he increased the vibrations. Angie opened her mouth to get more air. Jared was wicked to do this to her.

She tried to concentrate on anything but how the toys made her feel, but it was impossible when he turned them up. Her focus zeroed in on her core and the overwhelming heat and need that coursed through her. Her pussy and ass clenched around the toys while her clit pulsed.

"Don't fight your climax." His breath brushed her ear. "Let me see you come. Let me see your body go wild." As he said the last word, the bullet speed increased.

Wasn't it on high yet? Her toes curled, her fingers clenched and unclenched. She was on the verge, on that ledge, getting ready to fall over. Her mind tried to comprehend what was happening but couldn't.

Let go. In an instant, she flew over the cliff. She screamed as she climaxed, her pussy squeezing the toy, her ass clenching, and her clit doing a happy dance. It went on and on, but Jared didn't turn the toys off.

She'd barely started to relax when another climax hit and then another one. Her body twitched, and she moaned. Too much. She tried to call her safe word, but she couldn't speak. Her body went lax.

"Baby?" Jared's concerned voice penetrated the haze of pleasure.

Angie gave a weak grin as she floated on a sea of clouds. The toys were off now, but her body was so sated, she couldn't move, let alone speak.

"I see that grin. You're so beautiful when you let go." His lips caressed her shoulder and trailed down her spine. The fabric between her legs was released, and he removed the toy from her clit, then her pussy. Her breathing grew heavier as he removed the one from her ass.

"Easy, darling." He smoothed his palms over her ass. Her ankle restraints were removed and then the ones at her wrists. At last, the blindfold was removed.

She blinked several times until Jared's face came into view. His eyes were dark with desire and his body flushed. He also looked incredibly pleased with himself. Angie tried to push herself up.

"Let me help." His arm slid around her waist, and he lifted her off the bench.

"I…" She grabbed his shoulders when her feet touched the floor. Her knees wouldn't hold her up.

"I've got you." He lifted her and carried her over to the bed. Gently, he laid her down. "You are so beautiful." His lips brushed hers "Let me clean you up and then I'll massage your back and shoulders."

She realized how sore her shoulders and upper back were. Turning her head, she watched Jared leave the room, only to come back with a washcloth and a towel.

"Thank goodness I have a bathroom in here." With gentle strokes, he ran the washcloth over her body, being extra gentle with her pussy and ass. When he was done, he dried her off. "On your stomach."

With a groan, Angie rolled over. Jared straddled her legs and then began to massage her shoulders.

"That feels so good."

"You were tied up for a bit."

She opened her eyes and stared at him. "How long?"

"Hours." His magic hands skimmed down her back, up and down until she sank into the mattress. Jared shifted and began massaging the back of her thighs. Angie closed her eyes and let everything go. The level of satisfaction Jared could give her was frightening.

"Better?" he asked, climbing off her body.

"Yes." She rolled onto her side and stared at him. His cock was standing at attention, but then she suspected it had been hard all day. "Will you lie on your back for me?"

He gave her an inquiring look but flopped onto his back.

"Spread your legs."

"Are you forgetting who is in charge?"

She grinned at him. "Not at all." Angie stroked the outside of his thigh.

"Aren't you tired?" Was he concerned for her well-being? Seemed like it. Pleasure warmed her body.

"Not at the moment. Please?"

He parted his legs, and she climbed between them. His cock twitched. Angie cradled his erection in her hand, admiring the thick veins and the moisture at the head. She ran her finger over him.

"Angie," he started.

"*Shhh*. This big boy needs some attention." Leaning over, she swept her tongue over the head. Salty and spicy.

Jared groaned. "Baby, I don't know if I can take your mouth on me without coming."

"That's the idea." She opened her mouth and took him in. His body stiffened, but he didn't push her away. Angie took that as a good sign. Keeping one hand at the base of his cock, she began sucking him.

***

"That feels so good, sweetheart." Jared could barely talk. After watching her climax multiple times, his body was primed and ready. Hell, it had been for days. Jacking off had given him limited relief.

The last thing he expected was for her to suck him. He figured she'd want to cuddle a bit, then shower and eat. Instead, she made him even harder. He inhaled sharply as she hummed, sending delicious vibrations through his body.

He fought to keep his hands at his sides and not sink them into her hair to hold her in place. This was a gift she gave him. "Faster, baby." Jared couldn't help his words, and Angie didn't disappoint.

His balls tightened after too many days with nothing but his own hand for satisfaction. It wouldn't be long now. She stroked her tongue over his sensitive head, gathering his essence. His hips arched up.

Damn, she had a talented mouth. She drew him even deeper.

"Baby, I'm going to come." He had to warn her. Angie's gaze met his, and her eyes twinkled with mischief and—*holy shit*—she didn't stop. If anything, she sped up and used her other hand to stroke his base.

He ground his teeth together as his fingers tangled in her hair. His climax erupted. Spurt after spurt flowed into her luscious mouth, and she never stopped taking him in. Coming had never felt so good. She milked him and only released him when he lay limp on the bed.

His cock barely twitched as she shimmed up his body. "You taste like a man should—salty, spicy with a hint of earthy magic."

Jared slid his hands behind her neck and guided her lips down to his. He didn't care if he tasted himself on her lips. He had to kiss her. Now. To show her how much this meant to him. Their tongues mated, and his own salty taste had him pushing deeper into her mouth for more.

He drew her tongue into his mouth, then dove back into hers. He traced her teeth, the roof of her mouth before tangling with her tongue once again. He couldn't get enough of her.

Angie pulled away, panting. His lips trailed over her neck, then he rolled her onto her back. Without pausing, he covered one breast with his mouth, and his hand toyed with the other one, before he switched.

A tremor shook her body, and Jared lifted his head to see her watching him, her eyes gleaming with interest. "Your mouth is so erotic," she said.

He grinned, slipped an arm around her, then rolled them over. Angie was now cradled against his chest. "Rest." Her body needed some downtime after all their play.

"As long as you stay here with me." Her warm hand fluttered to his chest as she snuggled closer. He liked that she wanted to be close to him.

"There's no place I'd rather be." His words startled him, but they were true. He wanted nothing more than to lay here with her, even if they did nothing for the rest of the day but cuddle.

Funny, he wasn't usually the cuddling type, but with Angie, she kept proving him wrong. Her body relaxed in his hold. Jared shifted and found the sheet. He pulled it over both of them. She might get cold once she came down from her sensual high.

He yawned. Maybe a quick nap would be a good idea. Angie murmured something and moved closer to him. Jared tightened his hold on her, and she settled down. When he started down this road with Angie a few days ago, he figured it would be a way for both of them to scratch an itch.

But the longer he was with her, the more he saw the woman she hid from the world. A woman with sexual needs and a voracious appetite. He was happy to feed her whatever she wanted. For the first time in a long time, he was happy.

Chapter Seven

The next morning, Jared added up the columns again, and again, and again. Each time, the total came up different. "Damn it." He slammed his fist against the desk.

"Problems?"

He glanced up to see Angie standing in the doorway of his office in a pair of shorts and a t-shirt. And no bra. Damn.

"I thought I told you to take some time for yourself today?" They'd played a lot yesterday.

"You did, but I'm bored." She moved into the room with her hips wiggling just right to make his cock jump. "What are you having problems with?"

"My accounting system." Angie was a CPA, maybe fresh eyes could see what the issue was, because he couldn't find it.

"Let me take a look." She tried to nudge him out of the way.

"Have a seat." He snagged her around her waist and pulled her into his lap.

She giggled and positioned herself so her ass pressed against his unruly dick. She leaned forward, and he followed, resting his chin on her shoulder.

"*Hmm.*" Using the mouse, she scrolled up and down on the screen. "It looks like you've somehow mixed several accounts together."

"Possibly. Accounting was never one of my strong suits."

"Who does your taxes?"

"I have a guy in Sacramento. I just print everything out, hand it to him, and he does them."

Angie clicked her tongue. "Not good." She moved her fingers over the keyboard with precision, not his hunt-and-peck method. He watched, fascinated, and about fifteen minutes later she leaned back against him. "Done. Everything is back where it belongs."

"What?" He read the screen to see she was right. "How?"

"It wasn't that hard. I am a CPA, you know."

"Want a job?" The words slipped out naturally. Wouldn't it be nice to have an accountant on the ranch?

His thoughts scattered as she wiggled her ass over his growing erection.

"How about I help you while I'm here?"

She let him off the hook, but that didn't stop her from grinding against his cock. He nodded. Part of him was relieved, another part disappointed. "Let me go get my spare laptop, and we can get you set up." His hands framed her hips as he pushed her off his lap to her feet.

"Sounds good. I was..." A blush rose to her cheeks. "I was hoping we could play this afternoon." She had a flirty tone he'd never heard before. He was finally getting the real Angie.

Jared grinned. "Hold that thought. I'll be right back." He scooted his chair back, stood, and left the room.

***

Angie listened to Jared's retreating footsteps and slowly exhaled. He'd offered her a job? While she knew he wasn't serious, it still warmed her heart. Of course, she couldn't take him up on his impulsive offer, no matter how much she wanted to. The simple act of sitting in Jared's lap aroused her more than she thought possible.

If they worked together...

She shook her head. *Nope.* She had been here for the wedding, and now for two weeks. Unable to stand still, she wandered around his office, noticing the certificates and licenses on his walls.

There was no doubt in her mind he was a licensed sexual psychologist, but she didn't realize how much schooling it took. She paced until he came back into the room with the laptop and a robe over his arm. He set the robe in his chair.

"It will take me a few minutes to get this set up." He cleared off files from one side of his desk and dumped them onto an empty chair. He set the computer in the space he'd just cleared, pulled another chair over, and sat.

The clicking of computer keys filled the room. Angie realized how comfortable she was with Jared. That had never happened with any of the men at her job. She was always on edge around them, knowing they would bother her for help with the simplest tasks. With Jared, she didn't worry. He knew his stuff and, as he'd shown today, was willing to ask for help when he didn't.

"Okay, laptop is ready." He stood and walked over to her. "Now for your surprise."

"Surprise?"

He nodded. "Take your clothes off."

She stared at him, eager to see what he had planned. Angie pulled her shorts and T-shirt off.

"Everything."

Blowing out a breath, she removed her panties.

"You take my breath away every time." He tugged at her nipples, making them hard and seeking more attention. "Here's the first part of your surprise." He reached into his pocket and pulled out nipple clamps with jewelry. "Nipple danglers."

He slipped the first silver ring over her nipple before doing the same with the other. The crystals at the end jingled when she shifted from one foot to the other.

"Spread your legs."

She did what he said, and a shiver rolled through her when he knelt and parted her labia. Angie gazed at his dark brown hair, but she couldn't see what he was doing. Hard fought control prevented her from jumping when his fingers pinched her clit. There was more; something cool was placed over her clit. That wasn't quite right, it surrounded her clit, almost pinching it.

"*Ohhhh.*" As Jared removed his hand, her clit started throbbing, and there was a slight tug on her clit.

"Similar to the nipple danglers." He rose to his feet. "This one is called a clit caresser. It has several crystals hanging from it. Walk around the room."

Angie bit her lip. Could she walk? Desire filled her veins, and she took a step. She gasped as the toys moved. She took another step, and then another. Goodness. Pleasure shot from her nipples to her clit and back again.

"No pain? Not too tight?"

She shook her head, trying to control her breathing. *How the hell am I going to survive this?*

"Good." He crossed over and picked up the robe. "I know you'll worry that someone might come into my office, so you can wear the robe, but nothing else." Jared held it open and that meant she had to walk across the room to him.

Each step caused her blood to heat. By the time she reached him, her clit throbbed, and her pussy clenched. The soft fabric was slipped up her arms and over her shoulders. He tied the belt, making sure she was covered.

"Go sit down."

She forced her feet forward and sat in the chair he'd placed in front of the laptop.

"Scoot forward, please."

Angie adjusted her position. Jared reached between her legs and adjusted the toy, then straightened. He made sure her robe was closed. "Do you need a pillow for your back?" he asked.

"No, thank you." She usually sat forward when she worked.

"If you do, let me know, and I'll get you one. Otherwise, I'll let you get to work."

Get to work? Okay, she closed her eyes, willing herself to ignore the tingling between her legs.

***

It didn't take long before Angie began to fidget. Jared hid a grin. Her movements were only tormenting her more. She leaned back in the chair, then sat straight up, shifting from side to side. His toys were doing what he wanted.

"Problems?" he asked.

"Not with the accounting. You're all up to date."

"That was fast. I appreciate you working on the books." He pushed his chair back and waited.

"Ummm, Jared?"

"Yes, sweetheart."

"Can we go play, please?"

His dick swelled. She'd never asked before. "We can." He stood and held his hand out to her. He led her to the stairs and paused. "Take off the robe."

The fabric slipped from her shoulders, and her flushed body came into view. Jared sucked in a breath. Her beauty never failed to amaze him.

"Please, I need..." Her eyes closed.

"Easy, sweetheart." He leaned down and slipped two fingers into her pussy.

"Oh God, yes." Her hips shifted.

"I don't think you've been this wet before from just my toys." Not that it didn't make him happy.

"I'm sure there's a huge wet spot on the robe and the chair. Please, Jared, I need to come."

"Your wish is my command." He pulled his fingers free only to sweep her into his arms. Jared took the stairs two at a time. Once they were inside the playroom, he placed her on the bed and took off his clothes.

His cock twitched with anticipation. Climbing onto the bed, he knelt between her spread legs and stared at her. "Shall I leave the toys on?"

Her eyes grew wide. Part of him wanted to see how the toys would enhance sex, but he didn't want to cause her any pain or discomfort.

"I..." She blew out a breath. "Let's try."

He nodded. "Reach down and move the crystals out of the way. I don't want to snag them with my cock and hurt you."

Jared wanted to surge into her wet pussy. "I know we talked about it, but do you want me to use a condom?" There were some in the nightstand drawer.

"Only if you feel the need. As we discussed, I'm on the pill and at my last doctor's appointment everything was good."

"Same with me." Her consent meant so much to him.

"Please come inside me."

He lowered his body until the head of his cock was at her entrance. Slowly, he slid inside her. Oh, he didn't want to go slow; he wanted to take her hard and fast, but he wouldn't do that on their first time.

Her pussy tightened around him. "You're snug."

"Maybe it's because you're big."

Leaning over her, he brushed her lips with his as he pushed forward.

"Damn," she whispered.

"Am I hurting you?" He was prepared to pull out if he needed to. Her comfort was utmost in his mind.

"No." She wiggled her hips. "I want more."

"We'll get there." He flexed his hips, slipping deeper into her. Jared was aware he was a large man, and he didn't want to hurt her.

"Soon, please." She curled her legs around him. "I need you. I've needed you for days."

He grinned. "We've only been together six days."

"I don't care." She tightened her legs.

"Baby, loosen your legs."

"No."

"Don't forget who's in charge here."

She pouted but relaxed her legs.

Jared didn't give her time to be upset, he pulled back and thrust into her.

"*Ohhhh*." Her body quivered beneath his.

"So tight, but I'm loving it."

"Oh, yes. Love me. Take me to heaven."

He didn't respond. Instead, he flicked her right nipple with his tongue. Her body bucked against him as his tongue played with her nipple and the jewels. By the time he did the same with her other nipple, she was thrashing beneath him.

His own control hung on by a thread. He continued to play with her nipples as her fingers dug into his shoulders, and he kept a steady rhythm fucking her.

Her body shook under his. Her little mewing sounds made him smile. She was close. Angling his hips, he added pressure to her clit. Delicious tentacles of pleasure shot thorough his body. Angie cried out as her climax overtook her.

"That's it, baby." He flexed his hips. "Come for me."

Her nails dug into his skin with the next spasm of her body and the next. He didn't mind the pain. He gave one last thrust, his balls tightened, and his own climax over-took him.

Angie's body curled around him, her arms and legs holding him close. It was several minutes before he could even think coherently. So much better than his hand. So much. With care, he lifted his body from hers.

"No." she whispered.

"I'm not going anywhere." His lips brushed hers. He removed the nipple danglers, then the clit caresser. He tossed them on the nightstand before gathering her into his arms. Angie rested her head on his chest.

She snuggled close, and within a minute, she was making soft snoring sounds. His gut tightened. How would it feel to have Angie like this in his bed every night? He dismissed the thought quickly. His previous relationships didn't work out, so why would one with Angie?

He would enjoy their time together and move on. That's how it had to be. Even if he didn't want to let her go. His body could protest all it wanted. Angie was an angel who didn't need her wings clipped by his needs. He wouldn't do that to her.

Chapter Eight

Angie watched Jared as he checked and cleaned the horse's hooves the next morning. She'd agreed to go riding with him. She shook her head, wondering why she'd done that. It wasn't like she hadn't been on a horse before. Angie rolled her eyes. *Well, a pony in the park counted, didn't it?*

She liked the white spots on the horse's brown coat and enjoyed watching Jared as he worked. "Be right back." He left the stable only to return with his arms filled.

"What is that?" she asked. "I mean, I know it's a saddle, but it looks bigger than those I've seen before."

"It's a double saddle. This way we can ride together and enjoy the ride."

She didn't say anything as he settled the saddle on the horse, tightened the cinch, and checked it all out. Then he lifted two bags and laid them over the horse. "Ready?" he said.

"I guess." Angie walked over to the horse, who looked super big to her.

"Stand on the mounting block and put your left foot in the very front stirrup."

Taking a deep breath, she did and felt off balance. "I've got you." Jared's hands were at her waist. "Now, use your right leg as leverage and jump up. As I lift you, throw your leg over the horse."

"All right." She followed his instructions, grinning when she was seated on the horse. "I did it."

"You sure did." He slipped his foot into the rear stirrup and mounted behind her. His arms wrapped around her as he gripped the reins.

Angie understood the saddle then. There was more than enough room for the two of them. She snuggled against his chest. "How big is the ranch?" she asked as the horse began to move.

"About forty acres."

"Is that big?" She had no concept.

"Depends on your frame of reference. For a ranch that makes its money raising cattle and horses, no, it's pretty small. For us, it's perfect because we make our money off the other activities."

"How do you know it's small?" She rested her head on his shoulder, letting her body totally relax.

"I grew up on a ranch." He paused. "When my mom passed. I couldn't keep the ranch, but I promised myself one day I'd live on another one."

The sadness in his tone about his mom passing and losing his home tugged at her heart. Lifting her hand, she reached back and caressed his cheek. "You've made your dream come true, and I'm sure your mom is smiling down at you from heaven."

"You are a treasure." He took one hand off the reins, captured hers, and lifted it to his lips. He kissed her palm.

Delicious shivers of desire ran riot through her body. Unsure how to respond, she dropped her hand. "Tyler mentioned that you have some cattle."

"Yes. It's a small herd, only twenty of them. I have a manager up north who takes care of them. That part of the ranch is fenced off from the adult part."

"And the horses?"

"Tyler's job. We have several at the stables if guests want to ride on the trails. The trails are for riding and walking."

"Do you ever do normal dude ranch stuff?"

"Like what?"

"Hayrides, cattle round-ups, trail rides, sleep out under the stars... Stuff like that."

Jared nudged the horse to the trail on the left. "We can, but most of our clients don't care about anything like that. They can take trail rides whenever they want."

"What about sleeping under the stars?"

"I've never thought about it. None of the couples staying here have ever mentioned it. I'm sure we could arrange it, but most people like the comfort of their cabins."

"I bet. It's got to be hard to restrain someone in wide-open spaces."

"Not as difficult as you might think." He guided the horse between the gap in the trees and into a clearing.

"This is beautiful." Her gaze roamed over the clearing. The trees provided a natural shade, but didn't hide the light. It also looked like someone had cleared all the rocks and undergrowth. Jared stopped the horse and dismounted, then helped her down. "Can I help?"

He opened one of the large saddle bags. "Here." He handed her several blankets.

"Where do you want them?" He was prepared, and for some reason, that didn't surprise her.

"If you could spread them out over there." He gestured to an area that was shaded. "Layer them."

"Okay." Angie spread the blankets out in the area he indicated, her stomach doing summersaults. Jared was up to something; she could see the mischief in his eyes. "Finished."

"Catch." He tossed her several pillows.

Interesting. They were small pillows but still nice. She placed them on the blanket and turned back to see Jared pull a small leather bag out.

"Now for some fun."

His words snapped her to attention. Anticipation unleased a swarm of butterflies in her belly. *What was he planning?* She bit her lip.

"Take your clothes off."

She inhaled. "Jared, anyone could come along and see us."

"Are you afraid of being seen naked?"

"Yes." She crossed her arms over her chest and stared at him. "I have a feeling you're not planning a nice, normal picnic for us."

"You came with me of your own free will."

"Yes, but..." Had she subconsciously known what was going to happen? Maybe. Something clapped, and she jumped. Jared stood with his legs apart, a paddle in his hand. He slapped it against his palm...again.

Damn. There was that dark, dangerous Dominant.

He was serious about this.

"Yellow." The word slipped from her lips. Instantly, his demeanor changed.

"What is it, Angie?" he asked, moving over to her.

"I need to know that no one will stumble upon us."

He lifted his hand up and caressed her cheek. "No one is at the ranch but the construction workers, Vic, and his wife. The workers won't come out here. Vic and his wife are in Sacramento today. We're perfectly safe."

"Okay. Green."

His eyes blazed. "Clothes off."

She pulled her shirt over her head, and her breasts bounced free. Now she knew why he told her no bra. The cool air caressed her skin as she kicked off her shoes, then removed her jeans, underwear and socks.

"Go over to the blankets, arrange the pillows, and lie over them. I want your ass in the air."

She did what he said, but she couldn't quite relax. She listened for anything that might be out of place, but who was she kidding? She was a city girl. Everything was out of place.

"Because you used your safe word and told me your concerns, I'll be lenient about your punishment. Four smacks with the paddle."

Her eyes widened as he knelt next to her. Before she could ask him what he meant, the first swat stung her ass.

Then another and another. Heat filled her. The slight sting from the paddle turned into pleasure.

"So rosy." His fingers soothed over her ass. "Roll onto your back and spread your legs."

Angie took a deep breath. Using her arms and knees, she rolled onto her back. She gazed up at the tree branches that fanned out like tiny fingers against the deep blue sky and waited.

Finally, she turned her head to see Jared standing nearby, staring at her. A blush tinged her skin.

"Can you keep your legs spread or do I have to restrain you?"

She shivered. "I'll keep them apart." She couldn't allow him to restrain her. What if someone discovered them, even though he said they were alone? At least, unrestrained, she could grab some pillows to cover herself.

"All right. Close your eyes and let your other senses carry you."

Taking a relaxing breath, she closed her eyes and listened. A slight breeze ruffled the leaves, followed by a rustling of fabric. Was Jared undressing? She resisted the urge to peek.

"Being outside has its advantages." His breath brushed over her cheek. "Out here, I can play with you to my heart's content and not worry about business." His lips touched her nose, then cheeks and to her chin. "Best of all, we have fresh air and sunshine to decorate our world."

Jared trailed kisses down her neck, over her collarbone and shoulders. Light kisses, almost like air kisses, and very arousing.

Air rushed out of her lungs when he placed more butterfly kisses on her breasts, not lingering too long.

"Your lips should be marked with a danger sign." Her voice was breathless.

"Oh?" He smiled against her skin.

"Yes. *Danger... Lips attached to this man can seduce one with a single kiss.*"

"I like that." More kisses trailed over her belly and to the top of her thighs. "Keep your legs apart, sweetheart. I have something very special for you."

He lifted her legs and placed them on his shoulders. Her heart pounded. He blew against her slit, and she sighed.

"Pretty pink pussy." His fingers spread her apart. "And wet."

When his mouth covered her mound, she bucked against him. Hell, he thrust his tongue into her pussy. He swirled it around and... Angie forced herself to concentrate on what Jared was doing because something was different.

He pulled away. "You taste so good. Almost like cotton candy." He blew over her clit, causing shivers of anticipation to skim over her skin. "Ready for me?"

"I'm always ready." She almost hated to admit that, but it was true. Jared could arouse her with just a look.

"Keep your legs hooked over my shoulders." His hands gripped her hips.

"Damn!" Vibrations started in her pussy, and she almost lost her grip on his shoulders. "What the hell?"

His mouth was on her pussy, but something was vibrating as he licked her. Something small, yet powerful.

"Figure it out," he suggested.

His tongue slid over her clit and Angie almost lost it. *What the hell was going on?* It was like his tongue was a vibrator, but that wasn't possible. Her hips rose as he licked her. This was so wicked, so good, so decadent.

Her belly quivered as he continued to lick her, the tiny vibrations echoing in her body. Every nerve pulsed with anticipation. She wasn't going to last much longer.

"I'm going to come."

He didn't stop. Instead, he moved his tongue faster and harder. Higher and higher her tension rose, until he put his tongue directly only her clit.

Angie cried out as her orgasm rolled over her, her body shaking and her legs tightening around his head.

"I've got you, baby." His voice was rough as he lowered her legs from around his shoulders.

"That was wicked," she panted. He laughed and that's when she saw something on his tongue. "What is that?"

Jared pulled the item off his tongue. "This is a tongue vibrator. Now what shall I do to you?"

"Fuck me." She closed her eyes.

"Not yet." He stroked her overheated skin.

"Please?" Damn, now he had her begging. *What is he doing to me?*

"Let me try something different."

The rustling of material made her curious, but she didn't try to see what he was doing.

"Slight pinch."

Angie sucked in a breath as he placed nipple clamps on her hard nubs, and there was a chain that trailed over her stomach. What was he up to now?

His fingers were at her slit. "Prepare for another pinch."

Holy shit! He put a clamp on her clit. This was so much different from the dangler he had on her yesterday.

"Keep your eyes closed." Angie scrunched her eyelids as she was lifted and arranged onto his lap, his cock pressing against her entrance.

"Are you ready?"

"Oh yes." She wasn't sure how this was going to work, but she was game. Anything to get his hard cock into her. He thrust.

What the hell? She almost opened her eyes. Electric jolts went from her nipples to her clit. The chain must have something to do with that.

"Open your eyes, baby. See what I've done."

She did. Oh yeah, the chain was tight, and it pulled her nipples. As he moved, it also tormented her clit. The sensations increased her arousal.

"You're going to kill me."

"With pleasure." Jared leaned down and captured her lips. As he kissed her, somehow, he rose to his knees, and she sank farther onto his cock.

His palms cupped her ass, kneading them as he coaxed her into riding him. What was the saying—save a horse, ride a cowboy? Well, he might not be a cowboy, but she'd ride him anytime.

When had she become so wanton? Maybe it was always there, and Jared was the first man to bring it out in her. She rose and lowered herself onto his dick. It created delicious pressure against her clit, which in turn pulled the chain, and her nipples were tugged.

Too much. She rocked against him, increasing the pressure and her pleasure. She was going to climax again. She could feel it.

"That's it, baby. Come for me. Milk me."

His words ratcheted up her desire. She rose and fell rapidly until his cock twitched in her pussy. That was all she needed. She climaxed, and Jared groaned as he spilled himself inside her.

Panting, she laid her head on his shoulder. His fingers slipped between their bodies and he removed the clit clamp. Her pussy tightened around him, and she shifted. Tremors shook her body and rocked her against him.

The nipple clamps were removed, and she moaned, her body bucking as another orgasm swept through her. Jared held her until her body stopped trembling.

"You are fantastic." Holding her close, Jared lowered her onto the blankets and arranged them lying on their sides. Still connected. He nudged her head to his shoulder and cradled her close. "I want to bask in your body."

"Sounds good."

He chuckled and grabbed one of the pillows and slipped it behind his head. "Rest."

Angie closed her eyes and allowed herself to totally relax. Maybe later they could have another round of sex or play. She'd never enjoyed being with a man like she did with

Jared. She was going to miss him when they had to part ways.

A part of her was sad that she couldn't stay longer, but this wasn't meant to be. They'd agreed on two weeks, and she'd keep to that agreement.

***

Jared stretched carefully the next morning. He didn't want to wake Angie, but his muscles were protesting from yesterday's activities. He smiled. What fun they'd had in the clearing. Angie was as adventurous as he was.

Today he was going to work on that sexy ass of hers. He slipped from the bed and padded naked down the hallway to the playroom. Funny how he never spent the night in a woman's bed, yet with Angie, he'd done it several times.

Why didn't that bother him? Maybe because he'd finally found a woman who could enjoy his dominance. *But for how long?* Time was passing quickly, and he'd need to take what he could.

In the playroom, he began getting things ready for her. About an hour later, he watched as Angie started to wake. He wanted to climb back into bed with her, but he tamped down his need. There was a lot to do today.

"Good morning, sweetness." He kissed her when she opened her eyes.

"Umm, morning." Her hand curved around his neck. "I like being woken this way, but morning breath."

He chuckled. "I don't mind. But it is time to get up."

"All right," she groused. "Move." She pushed him in the chest. "Let me brush my teeth and clean up."

Jared slipped off the bed and helped her to her feet. "Do that. I have everything you'll need for today here." He gestured to the towel covered nightstand.

She stuck her tongue out at him and moved carefully to the bathroom. He liked this sassy side of her. When the water started, he lifted the towel and looked through what he had in store for her. After fifteen minutes, she walked back into the room, a towel around her body and her hair braided.

"Come sit down." He patted the mattress.

"What are you planning for today?" There was a slight tremor in her voice as she sat.

"Something to help you get ready for anal penetration." Her eyes widened. "Lie back, please." She did as he asked, then he lifted her legs. "Hold them over your head."

"Okay." He saw her hands trembling as she grasped her legs.

"Today, I want you to get used to having your ass and pussy filled at the same time." He poured lube on his fingers and massaged it into her puckered hole. With each pass of his fingers, he added more lube. Then he coated the toy and slipped it into her ass.

"Breathe," he coaxed. Angie obeyed as he pushed the toy fully into her ass.

She moaned.

"Okay?"

"Yes."

"Perfect." He rose and guided her legs to his shoulders. "Rest against my shoulders." Jared grabbed the dildo he wanted to use. He added lube to it, even though he was pretty sure he wouldn't need it and slid it into her pussy. "You were made for me," he whispered as the dildo was fully seated in her.

"I…" Her breathing hiccupped. "I can feel the plug in my ass rubbing against the dildo. But how will I keep them in place?"

"I have a harness for you." He lowered her legs from his shoulders and helped her off the bed. Grabbing the leather harness, he fastened it around her. "This will keep the toys in place today while we work. Oh, and you'll wear this." He lifted a piece of fabric.

"You've got to be kidding me." She swallowed. "There's next to nothing in that outfit; I'll be on total display."

"Yep. Turn around."

***

It wasn't easy, but Angie did as Jared requested, her insides spinning. He slipped the fabric around her waist.

"Take the two strings at the top and tie them around your neck while I do the rest."

She closed her eyes and then opened them as she grasped the ties and put them around her neck. Jared's fingers brushed her sides and back as he tied the rest of the outfit. Then he adjusted her breasts in the fabric.

His hands closed over her shoulders. "Come see how you look." He guided her over to the full-length mirror.

Angie blinked and then blinked again. This couldn't be her. Her skin was flushed, her eyes bright, and the black fabric covered her stomach. It was anchored under her breasts, and it cupped the side of her breasts, but left them bare otherwise.

Turning sideways, she saw the ties went around her waist, and there was a tiny bit of fabric between her legs that was tied to the waist ties.

"You can't feel it, but there is a G-string. Another time I'll have you wear this without the toys and harness."

A tremor swept through her. "I can't walk around like this."

"You can. There's no one in the house today but you and me. I will meet with the construction crew outside at eleven."

His palms covered her breasts and massaged them, before he pinched her nipples, sending electric shocks from her nipples to her clit. "Meet you for breakfast in ten minutes." He turned and left.

Angie groaned. How was she...

Here was the crux of the issue. She either trusted Jared to keep prying eyes away or she didn't. He'd been true to his word so far. She would have to take a leap of faith.

It was going to be a very long day.

***

By noon, Angie couldn't sit still. The toys were driving her crazy and keeping her on edge. And Jared... Damn the man. At random times, he'd tweak her nipples, or slap her ass cheeks, or kiss her until she couldn't think. But he seemed unaffected.

"Is something wrong? You keep wiggling."

She glared at him. "When are you going to take these toys out?"

"Soon, if you're a good girl."

"This isn't fair."

He grinned and her temper flared. "I never said I'd play fair. You do have your safe word."

Like she'd use it in this situation. Angie froze. She was actually enjoying what Jared was doing to her. How? She had no idea. But, for once in her life, she didn't have control, and she liked it. Angie clamped down on that thought.

Jared was demanding but fair, aggressive yet tender, and he matched her sexuality perfectly. *If only...*

Nope, she couldn't plan a future with him. They'd both agreed this was only for two weeks, but now, she wanted more.

She needed him. Angie bit her lower lip as an idea popped into her head. It was a dangerous idea, but she liked to play on the risky side. Standing up, from the desk across the room from Jared, she made her way to his desk. Without a word, she spun his chair toward her, leaned over, and slipped her fingers into his cotton shorts. Angie licked her lips as she freed his hard cock. Maybe not so unaffected as she thought.

"Angie." There was a warning tone in his voice, but she ignored him as she knelt and took him into her mouth.

God, he tastes so good. She ran her tongue over his shaft, loving the feel of it before taking him deep into her mouth.

"Damn it." His fingers tangled in her hair.

Yes! Triumph filled her. She wanted to do this. It made her feel good, and maybe she'd get off at the same time. While Jared had his hands on her head, he didn't try to control her in any way. He allowed her to lick and suck at her own pace. That was good, because she took him all the way to the back of her throat and swallowed.

"Fuck."

Her fingers found his balls and began caressing them. At that moment, Jared lost the battle. His essence filled her mouth as he shouted.

Power surged through her. Power that she could do this to him, make him come. She kept him deep in her mouth until he went limp. Angie lifted her head and kissed her way up his chest, to his neck, and when she would have bypassed his lips, his hand curved around her neck and pulled her mouth this.

She guessed he didn't mind tasting himself. His tongue tangled with hers as he held her tight. Then he broke the kiss. "You are incredible."

Angie smiled as she straddled him. Her body pulsed with need. "My turn."

His eyes twinkled with devilment. "Later."

***

The next three days passed faster than Angie wanted them to. The sense of freedom she had with Jared still amazed her. Nothing with him was taboo. He understood her. She could discuss what she wanted, her feelings, and her fantasies without fear.

He never made her feel like she was weird, or odd, or ashamed of her sexual needs. Not that he couldn't keep up with her. His appetite was just as strong as hers. Of course, there were those days where he'd tease her mercilessly, and she wanted to hit him over the head, but she did find ways to tease him as well.

She'd never been so in sync with a man, a lover, and she wasn't sure how she would give him up. They had four days left together. Four short days. Her heart tightened. Angie glanced up at Jared's relaxed face. She rarely woke before he did.

But she hadn't been able to control her excitement and anxiety about today. He told her last night, they would have anal sex today. A shiver slid through her body.

Jared's arms tightened around her, and their gazes connected.

"Good morning," she said.

"Morning." He brushed his lips over her forehead. "I can feel you thinking. Are you worried about today?"

Damn, he was so good at reading her. "A little."

"You don't have to do this if you don't want to. It's okay to make it a hard limit."

He was giving her a way out. So typical of Jared. He might be a Dominant, but he also took very good care of her. He was constantly reminding her to use her safe words if there was something she was uncomfortable with.

What she couldn't make him understand was that she didn't want to use the safe words. Each day, she anticipated what he had planned. Very little made her nervous or upset now. Even today, while she was a little anxious about anal sex, deep down, she knew it would be fine.

It wasn't like Jared hadn't prepared her. Each day, he'd put larger butt plugs in her, stretching her. And while the last one had been a bit uncomfortable, she still accepted it. "I want to do this."

"Wonderful." He gave her a soft kiss. "Shower, food, then we'll go into the playroom."

"We're not working this morning?" They'd been working side-by-side, and Angie found she really enjoyed the office time with Jared. Another thing she never experienced before. She'd always been a loner at work, and her co-workers came to her for help all the time, but with Jared, they were able to work together. The man was as intelligent as he was handsome and virile.

"No work. Today, I'm going to take my time." He slipped from the bed and stretched, his cock erect.

Angie swallowed. How different was this going to be from a butt plug? What if she let Jared down? She closed her eyes and took a deep breath before she climbed out of bed. Together, they walked into the bathroom. Another new thing with her—Jared enjoyed shower sex.

***

"Baby, you're too tense," Jared said two hours later. They'd made love in the shower, had a good breakfast, and chatted and laughed before they went to the playroom. Now, she was tense as a board.

"I know." What was wrong with her? Jared had been considerate all morning, and her body was ready for him, so why couldn't she relax. Was she afraid? She didn't think so, but her brain refused to listen to her body.

"Want to talk about what's going on?"

"If I knew, I'd tell you." She blew out a frustrated breath. "I don't know what's wrong."

"Maybe I'm going at this the wrong way."

"What do you mean?"

"Go get on the bed and put the wedge under your back. Spread your legs."

Her core clenched. Is this what she needed? To know she wasn't in control of what was about to happen? Angie arranged herself on the bed over the wedge.

She turned her head to watch Jared, and he strolled over to the cabinets and began removing restraints, lube, a small case, and a few other items she couldn't quite make out. He sauntered over to the bed and set everything down out of her sight.

"I can smell your arousal." He picked up the restraints and fastened them around her wrists and the other end to the headboard. "Close your eyes."

She did.

"Your nipples are hard."

"Yes." They were from the second he ordered her to get on the bed. Her body was primed for his commands, and she didn't mind it.

The sound of a bottle being opened made her flinch.

"Easy, love." His lips brushed over hers. "Just a little something to warm you up." His fingers were at her clit, rubbing it... No, rubbing something over it. "Now, let's make things a little more interesting."

Angie so wanted to open her eyes, but she wouldn't. She strained to hear what he was doing, but Jared gave nothing away. Her breathing increased as he slipped a finger into her pussy.

"Nice," he said. The finger was removed, and something round took its place.

A vibrating egg. Nothing new there, but then she realized another ball followed, and then another. She shifted her hips, and the toys rocked deep within her. She moaned as her clit began to warm.

"What do you feel?"

"My clit is heating up."

"I put pleasure cream on it, so you will feel everything I'm doing to you." He shifted on the mattress. "Get ready."

Before she could ask him what he meant, the balls in her pussy started vibrating. My god, what did he have planned for her?

"Talk to me."

"My body is tingling. My clit is pulsing so hard, and those balls are creating delicious heat in my body." She moved against the wedge, not that she could do much. Jared was between her spread legs and her arms restrained.

"What about this?" He covered one breast with his mouth, sucking her nipple deep before switching to the other one.

"I love it when you suck my nipples." Her pussy muscles tightened around the ball, and her clit begged for attention. "I want to touch you."

"Not yet." Cool air brushed her nipples as he blew on them.

Angie opened her mouth to get more air as the balls vibrated harder. She tried to buck her hips, but Jared held them, his breath wisping over her clit. "Please."

"I know what you want."

"Then give it to me."

He laughed. "With pleasure."

She cried out as he licked her clit. Damn man, he had the tongue vibrator on. Each lick not only made her clit hard and needy, it also sent tingles from her nipples to her pussy. "Not fair," she panted.

"Remember, I don't play fair."

She knew that, but damn it, why do this to her when she was restrained? Probably because he wanted to. Her body reacted to the balls and his licking. Her tummy tightened. How long could she hold out with him playing her body like this?

His mouth was relentless. He would suck her clit, then use his tongue on it. Even with him holding her hips, any tightening of her muscles caused the balls in her pussy to shift and send even more sensations through her body.

Angie could barely catch her breath, then he turned the vibrations up. The tide was building, and she wasn't going to be able to hold it back. "*Ahhh*, I'm going to come."

Her words must have spurred him on. He placed his tongue directly on her clit, pressing it against it. That's all it took. The waves crashed over her. She could die of pleasure right now and know she was thoroughly loved.

Funny how letting go of her control and letting him take the lead could result in so much pleasure.

***

Jared watched Angie closely. Her pale skin went from pink, to rose, and now totally flushed. Her submission was a gift to him, one he would never take for granted. She'd been tense before he gave her commands. He realized she needed it to feel safe and to let go of everything.

She was the only woman who'd ever accepted him for who he was: a sexual Dominant. She rarely balked at anything he did to her. While she never said *red*, she had used *yellow* when she needed him to slow down.

He removed the tongue vibrator and turned off the vibrating balls. He slipped the cock ring over his hard dick and then found the string hanging out of her pussy and pulled. The balls popped out one at a time. She groaned as each one came out.

He tossed them onto the nightstand and thrust into her.

"Jared," she cried out and opened her eyes.

He'd surprised her as he seated himself on the first thrust. "What do you feel?"

"Full. Full of you but there is something different." She scrunched her nose, which she always did when thinking hard.

Jared rotated his hips, and she gasped. With a grin, he tapped the controller on the bed.

"Oh shit." She groaned. "What do you have on?"

"A vibrating cock ring." He pulled back and thrust into her again, allowing the vibe to press against her clit.

"There's more than that."

"Well, there is the bullet that will tease us both and"—he rotated his hips—"a couple of small nubs to rub against your clit as well."

"You're going to kill me." She tugged at her wrists. "I want to touch you."

"No to the touching, and you might die of pleasure, but that's all I'll allow." He began moving in and out of her in long, leisurely strokes. The cock ring tormented him as much as it did her.

"My clit is on fire."

"That's the cream. It's making you sensitive to every touch."

"Oh, God, I'm going to—" Her body shuddered around his as she climaxed.

Jared held himself still as her pussy convulsed around his dick, letting her orgasm subside before he moved again. Each time she came, he let her body calm down before he continued. His cock was weeping.

Angie wrapped her legs around his waist. "Please, Jared. Take your pleasure. I want to feel it."

His strokes grew shorter and harder as the tension in his body built. He gave one last hard thrust and orgasmed. This triggered Angie into having another climax. Jared barely remembered to turn off the bullet as he rested his body against her. Thank goodness for the wedge and that he was on his knees.

Once he had his breathing under control and Angie stopped twitching underneath him, he pulled out of her wanting body. Disposing of the cock ring and bullet, he released her arms and picked up the bottle of lube.

"Onto your stomach." He helped her roll over on the wedge until her ass was in the air. "Pretty." He slapped her globes before lubing up his fingers. Slowly, he spread the lube around her ass.

The plugs had done their job. She was ready for him. Jared wiped his fingers off on a towel and slid on a condom. Keeping the lube close, he pressed the head of his dick against her ass. "Suck in a breath and push out." Normally he would need more recovery time, but his cock didn't seem to care.

She did as he asked, and when her ass flexed, he pushed forward. Inch by inch, he worked himself into her ass until he was fully seated. He groaned as she tightened her muscles.

***

Angie could barely breathe. Jared's cock was buried in her ass. While there had been a little pain, nothing prepared her for the feeling of fullness that enveloped her.

"How are you doing?" he asked, his breathing labored.

"I'm good."

"No pain?"

"A little burning at the beginning, but nothing I couldn't handle." She closed her eyes and concentrated on her body and his. "Please. Show me how good this is."

"Your wish is my command."

He pulled back and then slid back in. He did this in long, slow strokes. Her clit was on fire again. Her pussy muscles kept tightening.

"You're so tight."

"And you're so big." His thrusts were quicker now. "Please!" She didn't know what she was begging for, but she needed something. Another orgasm maybe?

"I don't want to hurt you."

"You won't. I want you to do this. I'm ready."

"Hold on, baby."

His strokes were harder and shorter. Her fingers curled into her palms as her body tingled with the unknown.

Angie used her knees and rose, meeting him on his downward thrusts. She never knew anal sex could feel so good. Her pussy clenched. Jared shifted and then his fingers were at her clit.

Her orgasm roared through her like a freight train, and she screamed his name. Jared wasn't far behind, and he shouted her name. His body trembled above hers as he climaxed. They collapsed against the wedge.

Jared's lips caressed her ear. "You are so beautiful, so damn sexy." He lifted his body off of her and popped out of her ass.

She was wasted and had no idea if she could move or not. Jared climbed off the bed, and she assumed he disposed of the condom. They next thing she knew, he lifted her off the wedge, and it was pushed away. Then she was in his arms, lying against his chest.

Her entire body throbbed with his loving. She took a deep breath and let it out. Her ear was against his chest, and she could hear his unsteady heartbeat. He'd been as affected as she had. She smiled. They'd both gotten their pleasure, and while she'd come more than he had, she had no doubt in her mind that he was happy.

It was too bad they had so little time left together, because Jared had spoiled her for other men.

Chapter Nine

❤

Jared surveyed his handiwork on the back porch the next morning. The loungers were set up, food laid out, now all he needed was Angie. They only had a few days left and then she'd leave. He wanted her to stay. A first for him. When he made this agreement with her, he never expected to find a woman who would relish his control. He walked into the kitchen and poured her a cup of coffee.

As he mounted the stairs to wake her, he realized he didn't know a lot about her life. Today, he would fix that.

Angie had to have her morning coffee, and he had no problem taking it to her. Inside her bedroom, he crossed to the bed and waved the coffee under her nose. She stretched but didn't open her eyes.

"Morning, sweetness." He brushed a kiss over her soft lips.

"Morning." Her eyes opened and she pushed herself up as he straightened. He placed the mug in her outstretched hand.

"*Mmm,*" she purred as she blew on the coffee before taking a sip. "I love waking up this way."

Jared's heart leapt. Love. The word echoed in his head. Women had told them they loved him before, only to walk away when they couldn't handle his brand of sex. But Angie was different, he reminded himself. The past week and a half told him that. She didn't balk at anything he wanted to try.

There were only a few things she refused to do a second time. One was using the cane; she agreed to try it, but after two swats, she'd called out *yellow*, telling him she wasn't into that kind of pain for pleasure. The other was being restrained on the kneeler. When she called *yellow* again, they'd had a long talk. She finally explained that it made her feel too vulnerable, too helpless. Jared understood, and he admired her honesty with him. That's what relationships were about.

Is that what I have with Angie? A relationship? It had been way more than sex. They'd worked together in his office, ate most of their meals together. Heck, he took her morning coffee more often than not.

Jared pushed those thoughts away. He'd think on it another day when his head was clearer.

"Your eyes are sparkling," Angie remarked. "What do you have planned for today?"

"Some fun."

Her mug was almost empty. He really must have been lost in his thoughts. He held his hand out to her as she placed her cup on the nightstand. "Go shower while I find the right clothes for you."

Angie groaned as he pulled her to her feet. "Nothing too revealing, please. We almost gave that construction worker a heart attack."

Jared slapped her ass as she walked by. "Yeah." They'd been playing outside when one of the workers stumbled upon them. The worker had taken a wrong turn and ended up at the back of the ranch house. The kid, barely twenty-one, babbled out his apologies, then tripped over his own feet trying to get away.

Later, the construction manager apologized to Jared and Angie for the accident and promised none of the workers would come close to the ranch house again. Angie thanked him, but her face was flushed the entire time.

Jared didn't blame her, but the outfit hadn't been that revealing, nothing the worker wouldn't have seen at the beach.

A topless beach.

Jared had spent the afternoon with Angie, assuring her that the kid wasn't traumatized and making sure she wasn't upset.

Going over to her closet, he pulled out a colorful skirt and a white T-shirt. Then he ran to the playroom and pulled out the toys he wanted her to wear today. When he returned, she was walking into the bedroom, staring at the clothes on the bed.

"At least, I won't give anyone a heart attack."

Jared chuckled. "I have some items for you to wear underneath." He held up a thong.

Angie puffed out a breath. "You're going to tease me again today."

"You bet I am." Jared stepped up to her and knelt. She lifted one foot and then the other, and then he slipped the thong up her legs. "Spread your legs."

He finished pulling the material up until it was snug around her waist. Using his fingers, he traced the thong between her butt cheeks, then to her pussy. Her hips shifted when his fingers took the two rows of beads that made up the front of the thong and adjusted them.

"No vibrator this time, but the beads will stimulate you." He tightened the thong. "How does that feel?"

"Sinful."

Jared chuckled. He stood and picked up another toy, then slipped it over her neck. "This is a great piece of jewelry." He ran the silver chain down her neck until the ends hung below her breasts. "These"—he held up two silver drops—"are very special."

He slipped the lambskin leather loop over her already hard nipples and tightened the loop. Once that was done, he released the sliver drops.

Angie gasped.

"I love these." He flicked one of the drops with his finger before he stepped back to admire his handiwork.

"Why is it I always have to wear the jewelry? Why can't I put some on you?"

"One day." He kissed her. "Go ahead and dress." Jared walked away. The idea of her putting a cock lariat or other such items on him had his dick straining against his pants. He wasn't opposed to the idea.

Once she finished dressing, he took her hand and led her downstairs and onto the back porch. He'd already set everything up. Jared stretched out on the lounger, legs on either side, and patted the space between them. Angie sat and leaned back against his chest.

"Let's chat," Jared suggested. "Tell me more about yourself. Where did you grow up?"

***

Angie took a deep breath. She didn't talk much about her family. "After I was adopted, Visalia, in the Central Valley." The feeling of dread when she talked about her adopted family was absent. *Interesting*.

"What made you move to San Francisco?"

"I wanted the big city and bright lights." Her stomach tightened when she remembered moving. Her adopted family was great, but they didn't have a lot of money. She only had a couple changes of clothes and money she'd saved up from summer jobs.

She'd come a long way from that scared eighteen-year-old. "What about you? Where was the ranch you grew up on?" It was only fair that she learn about him too.

His arms tightened where they rested around her waist. "I grew up in Orland. It's a couple hours' drive from here."

"Another small town."

"Yes, but I loved it."

"I bet. You could be top dog." She was enjoying this laid-back relaxed chat with Jared, even if every little movement ratcheted up her need for him.

He laughed. "So to speak. I've always liked to be in control. I know my limits in public situations, though." His lips brushed her temple. "How did you become a CPA?"

"I like numbers." She shifted. The beads on the thong were driving her a little crazy. "I was good at math, so I took a clerical position at a firm, attended night classes, and worked my way up."

"And succeeded."

"Yes." She sighed. *Maybe succeeded too much.* If success meant having to make all the decisions, she'd rather have failed. She was tired of making all the decisions. This time with Jared had been a blessing. Her mind already felt freer than it had in a long time. "Where did you go to college?"

"San Francisco State."

"Is that where you met Tyler?" Becca had told her about meeting Tyler in college.

"Yep. We had a class together, but we didn't meet up again until a few years after we both graduated."

"And you decided to open the ranch?"

His fingers skimmed over her abdomen. "When we ran into each other at a conference, we went out for drinks. We were playing catch up, and Tyler expressed an interest in opening a dude ranch. I'd just put a down payment on the land for what you see today. Tyler's eyes lit up, and I asked him if he wanted to be my business partner."

"Were you always planning on it being an adult ranch?" She tilted her head so she could see his face.

"Well, the conference Tyler and I attended was about sexual preferences. I realized there was no safe place for couples to explore their sensuality. I told Tyler my idea."

"And Quick Silver Ranch was born." She'd never heard Jared so animated as he was when he talked about the ranch. This place was very special to him.

"It took some time, but we eventually pulled it off." His voice held pride, and she liked it. He should be proud of what he and Tyler had accomplished.

She brushed a kiss over his chin. "How long before you became a runaway success?"

"What makes you think we're a success?"

Her laughed filled the air. "Since I've been looking at your accounts, I know how much you're making. Not that I care. But knowing you, the ranch could only be a success."

"It's amazing what word of mouth will do." He brushed the undersides of her breasts with the pads of his fingers, careful not to disturb the tear drops.

She pressed her ass against his groin.

"Are you wet, my sweetness." His lips were against her ear.

"Yes." Of course she was. He made sure of it.

"I can see your nipples straining against the fabric of your t-shirt."

"Someone put a toy on them."

"And the bead thong?"

"Teasing me. As I'm sure you wanted." She wiggled her ass against his erection. "You're hard."

"If you keep that up, I'm going to burst." He gently bit the lobe of her ear.

Her heart pounded. Their time was almost up. Was this going to be the good-bye speech?

"There's one of your fantasies I haven't fulfilled yet."

"Oh, which one is that?" He'd done so many things, a lot of them she'd never even fantasized about.

"You with two men."

Her blood heated. They'd talked about it in the beginning, but she hadn't really thought about it, since the ranch was closed, and there was no one else around. "What did you have in mind?"

His hands covered hers where they rested on her belly. His skin was cool. "There's a club in Sacramento I'm a member of."

"A gentleman's club?" She couldn't quite picture Jared going to a place like that. He was too sexual to sit and watch women strip.

"Not really." He shifted. "You know I like my sex a little rough and kinky."

"Yes, and in case you haven't noticed, I'm enjoying that side of you too."

"Which makes me happy." His lips caressed her cheek. "The club is owned by a friend, and it's a BDSM club."

"Oh." That was the only word she could think of.

It did make sense. Jared needed to have an outlet where he could explore his needs. He'd mentioned one night that it had been some time since he'd been with a woman who enjoyed sex like she did.

"Gabe is a friend, and I've already spoken to him. If you're agreeable, we will go to the club tomorrow. Gabe will be our third."

Angie closed her eyes. Excitement filled her—along with apprehension. How would it feel to have another person with them? Would they play in the club? Would others be watching?

"I can feel your anxiousness. Gabe will know your safe words and the rules around our ménage."

She nodded, and her fingers entangled with his. "Tell me what the ménage will entail." One thing she'd learned in her time with Jared was if she asked him questions, he would answer her.

"Anything you want. You'll have two men to worship your body, two sets of hands caressing you, two sets of lips to kiss and lick every inch of your body."

Each word increased her arousal. "Will Gabe want to fuck me?"

"Only if you want." His lips caressed her temple. "How would you feel having another man in your mouth?"

"That might work." She could see Jared getting very worked up as she sucked another man, and she didn't think it would be too bad.

"Would you allow him to take your ass while I fucked you?"

Angie stiffened. She hadn't thought about that. Two men, two cocks... Oh the possibilities, but still, she was hesitant. "I'm not sure."

"It's okay." His breath brushed her cheek. "We can play things by ear. You have your safe words, and we will stop the instant you call it out."

"Will you use toys?"

"Oh, yes." She could feel his smile against her skin. "Toys. Lots of them. We'll play with your body for hours until you're screaming for us to make you come."

What little apprehension Angie had left, she pushed away. If she passed up this opportunity, she'd always wonder what could have been. "Let's do it."

Jared turned her face to his, and they kissed deeply. Before she knew it, she was straddling his hard erection. Jared's fingers worked her T-shirt up and over her head.

Her sensitive nipples rubbed against his hair-roughened chest. When had he removed his shirt?

"As much as I like these"—he played with the tear drops— "it's time for them to go." He loosened the fastening and pulled the necklace off.

Slipping his fingers inside the waistband of the skirt, Jared began to slide it down, and Angie helped him by lifting herself up. When it reached her ankles, she kicked it away, then found the fastening of his jeans.

"Easy, baby." He covered her hands with his.

"I want you."

"You can have me, but let's not rush it."

***

Jared couldn't sleep, but he didn't want to get out of bed. He enjoyed holding Angie, feeling her warm body cuddled up to his. He glanced at the clock and bit back a groan. Three in the morning. While he'd slept for a few hours, he also knew what was keeping him awake.

The threesome with Gabe.

It wasn't that he didn't want to fulfill Angie's fantasy. He did, but her hesitation made him wonder if she really wanted this. Or was she trying to please him? There was also the big elephant in the room: he'd been the third with Becca and Tyler. Did Angie even know about that?

She was close with Becca, and it was possible Becca told her about it, but he didn't know. Angie never said anything or indicated she knew.

She shifted in her sleep, and he tightened his arms around her. He needed to take things one step at a time. In the morning, he'd tell her about Becca and Tyler. It would give her an out if she needed it. He wasn't willing to risk Angie not enjoying herself. She meant way too much to him, and he wouldn't see her hurt.

Chapter Ten

♥

Friday afternoon, Angie paced around the back porch. At lunch, Jared had told her he'd like to talk with her and asked her to meet him there. He'd been quiet all morning, even while they worked. Plus, no playing this morning. No matter how many times she tried to initiate something.

Jared would just smile, drop a kiss on her forehead, and step away. She was starting to feel like an old girlfriend. Except her body didn't feel that way. No, it throbbed with need and desire. She was falling for him. He'd wormed his way into her heart. She'd found a man who could keep her satisfied in the bedroom and out of it.

The problem: She was leaving Sunday. Jared hadn't given her any indication that he wanted to make a go of a relationship. She'd gone into this with her eyes open. Two weeks of sexual satisfaction.

Uncertainty crowded in on her. Looking out at the trees behind the house, she wondered if she'd done something wrong. Was it possible Jared didn't want to do the threesome? Or maybe he was tired of her? Her fears chased each other in her brain.

"Come sit down."

Angie jumped. She hadn't even heard him come outside. His tone was soft, and her heart clenched. She blew out a breath and took a seat. Jared sat in the chair facing her and reached out and took her hands. His were icy.

"Jared, what's wrong?"

"I have something I need to tell you."

She was sure her heart had stopped beating as fear shot through her veins. She should be used to rejection by now. Hell, her parents had rejected her, and so had many foster families, until her last one. Not to mention boyfriends. Apparently, Jared wasn't any different.

"You want me to leave, don't you?" Might as well come out and say it. Rip the Band-Aid, off so to speak.

"Hell, no." His hands tightened around hers. "You may want to after I tell you what I need to."

Angie frowned. Was she reading him wrong? "Tell me, please."

***

Jared swallowed the lump in his throat. Angie had a right to know. "You know Becca spent a week here at the ranch with Tyler."

"Yes, I'm the one that bought the trip for her and encouraged her to take it."

"How much did she tell you about her time here?" The lead ball in his gut grew bigger.

"Everything." She tilted her head and stared at him.

"Did she tell you about her threesome?" His heart pounded as he waited for her answer.

"Yes." Her fingers tightened around his.

"I was their third."

"I know." She leaned forward and brushed a kiss over his lips. "Becca told me about it."

"She did?" Now why did that surprise him? Maybe because Becca didn't seem as open as Angie was.

"Of course." Angie grinned. "Becca is no fool. She saw my interest in you the second I saw you. She wanted to let me know about it."

"It doesn't bother you?" What was he thinking? If it had, she wouldn't have agreed to spending time with him on the ranch.

"I really never thought about it after Becca told me." She cupped his cheek. "Jared, I'm glad you were there for her and Tyler. Becca needed someone like you to be part of the threesome."

He gazed at Angie, relief filling every fiber of his being. "I was worried you'd be upset."

"Becca's my best friend. She needed you for that one time. I'm okay with it because I didn't know you at the time, and Becca told me it was a one-time thing."

"You're unbelievable." He put his hand behind her head, pulled her to him, and kissed her hard.

"Can we play now?" she asked when he released her mouth.

"No." He stood and helped her to her feet. "Anticipation." Jared was relived she was okay with him being with Becca.

"Screw anticipation. I want you." Her fingers dipped into the waistband of his pants.

"I said no, Angie." He captured her hands. "You will listen to me on this. No sex until tonight." Stay strong. As much as he wanted to take her to the playroom, he wouldn't.

"I'm going to pay you back for this."

"I can't wait to see you try." She would try, but she wouldn't succeed not with what little time they had left together.

"Fine." She huffed and stomped into the house.

Jared grinned. He loved her feistiness. He loved a lot of things about Angie. *Don't think like that.* He might want Angie to stay, but he knew, in reality, it wouldn't happen.

***

Jared stared at the nearly empty road as they dove to Sacramento. They'd been on the road for thirty minutes and Angie's silence put him on edge. He'd almost forgotten to tell her to pack a bag, and when he did, all she did was glare at him. The traffic was almost non-existent, which was a bit surprising. It was only five in the evening. He glanced over at Angie. Her body language was closed, but there was also some nervousness. She was twiddling her fingers.

"You don't have to do this," he reminded her. If she was having second thoughts, he wanted her to know it was okay if she changed her mind. Even though they'd discussed it at length, he would never pressure or force her into something she didn't want to do.

"Do what?"

"The threesome." He took a deep breath. "Say the word and I'll turn the car around." Usually, he'd do as he thought was right, but there was something about Angie that had him asking her.

"Isn't your friend expecting us?"

Of course, she'd worry about that. "Yes, but I can call him and explain."

"Are you chickening out?"

The anger in her voice surprised him. "Why are you angry?"

"You tell me, oh mighty therapist."

Jared was glad he'd driven this stretch of road a million times. He took the next off ramp and drove down the two-lane road until he could pull off without impeding traffic. Not that there was any. He'd chosen this road for a reason. There was nothing here. All he'd ever seen here were big rigs, but he hadn't seen one since they got on the road.

"What the hell is wrong with you?" He turned off the ignition and looked at her, his own temper starting to brew.

"Me? I'm not the problem. *You* are, buster."

"Really?" He stared at her, but she refused to meet his gaze.

"Yes. You've aroused me, seduced me, teased me, and fucked me. I get you like denying me orgasms and I've been fine with it up until now. The one day I want you to take the edge off, you say no. I want to climax."

She wanted to control this situation. Why hadn't he seen it before? The little minx was going to understand he was the one in control. "Get out of the car."

Angie crossed her arms over her chest and stared out at the empty road.

Jared took a deep breath and pushed down his anger. She was baiting him, and damn if he wasn't rising to it, in more than one way. "Get. Out. Of. The. Car."

Something in his tone must have signaled her that he was out of patience. Angie released her seatbelt and opened the door.

Jared was out in a flash and at her side when she climbed out. Without a word, he took her by the arm and led her to the back of his vehicle. Opening the trunk, he took out a heavy blanket he kept there for emergencies. He slammed the trunk and laid the blanket over the trunk.

"What are you doing?" There was a hint of uncertainty in her voice.

"Lay on your stomach."

Her posture screamed defiance. Jared waited.

"Make me." The gleam in her blue eyes caught him off guard. She was enjoying this. Angie wanted him to lose control. She knew exactly what buttons to poke and had done it well. He wouldn't disappoint her, but he'd maintained his control.

Jared snagged her wrists and pulled them behind her back as he maneuvered her until her arms were caught between her body and his. "Are you sure you want to push me like this?"

She didn't answer. "Fine." He released her. Instead of him removing her clothing, he was going to have her do it. Angie needed her Dominant. "Remove your blouse, jeans, and panties."

"Someone could see us."

"You should have thought of that before you challenged me." He crossed his arms over his chest.

She glared at him, but she obeyed him. Did she even realize that? She acted like she wanted to be in control, but she actually didn't. Angie had strong submissive traits he'd recognized early on.

Angie leaned against the car to take her shoes off.

He stopped her. "No. The shoes stay on."

"I can't remove my jeans with my shoes on."

"True. You can take them off to remove your clothing but then put them back on."

She flashed him another glare but did exactly as he instructed. Jared took her clothes from her, folded them, and placed them out of harm's way. "Now, bend over the car."

The heels she wore put her at the right height. Leaning over her, he placed his legs between hers, pushing hers outward as he lifted her arms up and over her head.

"You've been a bad girl," he whispered in her ear. Her body shuddered beneath his. "Don't move."

Jared stood, removing his weight from her. Her face was turned to the side, eyes closed, mouth open, and her body flushed. He stepped back and admired her pert ass. He'd give her what she wanted, but on his terms. He slapped her ass.

"Ouch!"

He pressed his hand on the small of her back as she started to rise. "I told you, you've been a very bad girl, and bad girls get spankings." He smacked her again and again in rapid succession. When he paused to rub her ass, she moaned. Oh, yes, his Angie was enjoying this.

***

Angie couldn't believe she'd challenged Jared. Now, she was naked on the side of the road, and he was spanking her. But damn, if the spanking didn't feel good. Her pussy clenched with each strike, her nipples hard pebbles against the blanket.

A part of her was aware she wanted this. She'd been walking a tightrope all day and kept seeing how far she could push him. Well, she'd pushed him right over the edge.

Her clit throbbed, and she hoped the spanking would send her over the edge, but no. Jared wasn't spanking her hard enough. His swats were almost soft, and each time he caressed her hot ass, her body came down off the peak.

Had he figured out her game? She opened her eyes, and while all she saw was the foliage on the side of the road, she heard Jared's labored breathing. Was he as aroused as she was? He pressed his hips between her legs, forcing them wider. His hard cock pressed against her ass.

"Was this what you wanted, baby?" he whispered.

"Please." She tried to buck against him. "Take me."

"Are you wet?"

His words sent a shaft of heat through her veins. "Find out for yourself." *Where did those words come from?* Maybe because she was frustrated. Or, maybe, because she was tired of him playing with her body and emotions.

"*Hmmm.*" She felt him shift position. Jared traced a finger over her slit, causing a shiver of anticipation to flow over her. "You're dripping. From a little spanking."

Angie wiggled her hips, trying to get him to penetrate her with his finger. It wouldn't take much to send her over. But he pressed hard against her and removed his hand.

"Straighten up and put your pants back on."

A light breeze brushed over her body, and she shivered as she bit back a curse. He was doing it again, getting her all hot and bothered and not finishing her off. She straightened and reached for her panties.

"Just your pants, no panties."

Taking a deep breath, Angie picked up her jeans. The denim material would tease her for the rest of the ride.

"Do it."

Fuck. Taking off her shoes, she slipped them on. She grimaced when they rubbed against her slit as she put her shoes back on.

"Good girl. Put your shirt on and get back into the car."

His voice was stern, but when she looked at him, his eyes were dancing with desire and delight. He wasn't angry. She hid a smile. Slipping her shirt on, she made her way back to the passenger side and climbed in.

Her clit continued to throb. She almost wanted to rub herself against the coarse material and get herself off. But if she did that, it would get her into more hot water with Jared. *Damn, this was going to be a long drive.*

Jared watched her fasten her seatbelt, then leaned into the passenger side and kissed her hard. "Top from the bottom and I'll give you more than a light paddling." He straightened. "You will not come."

The door slammed, and Angie huffed. Jared opened the back door, threw the blanket and her panties on the seat, then climbed behind the wheel. He turned to her.

"When we get to the club, I'm going to enjoy pleasuring you so much you won't know which direction is up. You'll come so much and so often you'll beg me to stop. That's when Gabe will join us, and we'll start all over again. You wanted me out of control? Well, now you'll have it."

Angie closed her eyes and leaned her head back. This was out of control? She would say he was still in control. Was she reading him wrong? She glanced at him as he made a U-turn and headed back to the main road.

Well, she had wanted him out of control. She sighed. Jared would never hurt her or push her too far. She trusted him to know exactly what she could take, and if she needed it, she had her safe words.

Tonight was going to be fun.

***

When Jared finally stopped the car at a large metal gate, Angie shivered as she stared at it. They'd been on this back road for about fifteen minutes, almost two hours from the ranch. Forests surrounded the area. A person could get lost out here.

He rolled down his window, punched in a code on the keypad, and waited. After a minute, the black gate opened, and they drove through.

"Xavier's is a private club, and only those with the right code are allowed in. There are also cameras around the entire estate to keep unwanted visitors out."

"Does that happen a lot?"

"Not that I'm aware of. It's more of a safety precaution."

Angie gasped as a huge mansion came into view. "The place is big." It didn't look like a BDSM club, but then she'd never been inside one.

"Gabe owns all the land nearby so no one can build."

"Like your ranch?"

"Yes. But the club is nothing like the ranch." He pulled into the circular driveway. The waiting valets opened the doors as soon as the vehicle came to a stop. "Good evening, sir, ma'am."

"Good evening, Nigel." Jared dropped the key into the man's palm, then helped Angie out of the car. "Our bags are in the trunk. Gabe will know what room we're in."

Valets? This seemed more like a high-class hotel than a club. Jared held her hand as they walked up the stairs. Angie admired the old style of the house, columns and a huge, wrap-around porch.

"Welcome to Xavier's, sir, ma'am," a uniformed man at the door said. He grasped the door handle and pushed the door open. "Enjoy your evening."

"Thank you." Jared guided her into the house.

The foyer was open with high ceilings. The paintings on the walls made Angie feel like she was in an art gallery. Jared kept moving to a corridor and into another room.

She stopped in her tracks. The room was big. Along the back wall was a large bar area, and the rest of the room was filled with sofas and overstuffed chairs, some of them occupied.

Occupied? Interesting choice of word. In one chair, a man was enjoying a blow job. On a sofa, there was a man and two women. The women were almost nude as he fondled their breasts. There were two couples on another sofa, all fondling each other. There were other people in the room, but Angie dropped her gaze.

They hadn't discussed others watching them. She swallowed. Her heart pounded, and her gut clenched. She was about to ask him when a couple caught her eye.

The man was stroking the woman's neck just above a silver choker with several tiny hearts on it. As his fingers moved over the metal, they gazed into each other's eyes, totally oblivious to everyone else in the room. Love shined from them, and Angie wondered if she'd ever find a man to stare at her like that. *Would Jared ever look at me like that?*

"It's early. Later, the room will be full," Jared said, pulling her attention back to him.

"They don't mind people watching them?"

"This is the gathering room," a male voice chimed in.

Angie turned her head. *Oh my.* Her hand fluttered to her chest. The man was as tall as Jared but had jet-black hair and a swarthy complexion that spoke of Mediterranean ancestry.

"I'm Gabe." He glanced at Jared, who nodded, and then Gabe held his hand out to her.

"Angie." She placed her hand in his and wondered about the nod. It really didn't matter. This was the man who was going to be the third in their threesome.

"I'm pleased to be of service." He kissed the back of her hand and turned to Jared. "You are a lucky man."

"Damn right." Jared took her hand from Gabe's.

Gabe's eyes twinkled in the light. "As I said, this is the gathering room. The members will gather here before moving on to more private rooms."

"Private rooms?" No wonder this place was so big.

"This room is for meeting up, getting to know each other, and foreplay. No intercourse or play that could result in bodily fluids can happen here. A member must take sex or heavier play into a room."

Angie nodded, feeling slightly better that she wouldn't be on display. But she kept her eyes on the men and not what was going on in the room. "And is there always someone in this room?" she asked.

Gabe grinned. "Yes. Many of the members are exhibitionists." His gaze turned to Jared. "Per your request, I've prepared room forty-five for us."

"Shall we?" Jared slipped his arm around her waist as they followed Gabe down a hallway to two guards at the staircase.

"Guards?" she asked.

"Yes. We make sure only those who signed up for a room are allowed up. Plus, it helps some of the newer members know what is off-limits," Gabe answered.

Angie nodded. "How many rooms do you have?"

"Eighty, each designed differently." He glanced down at her feet. "If you have an issue walking up the stairs, we do have an elevator."

"I'm good."

Gabe nodded. "There are twenty-five on the first two floors and fifteen on the next two." They paused on the landing. "This is the green floor for novices." Gabe pointed out the green sign before they continued up.

"You're not a novice any longer," Jared whispered in her ear.

"This is our floor." Gabe gestured to the long hallway and guided them left.

Angie noticed the color on this floor was purple. "What are the colors of the other two floors?" She was curious.

"Blue and Red." Gabe stopped at a door where a burly man stood. "Rico, this is Jared and Angie. This will be their room tonight. I will be joining them later." Gabe turned to her. "Please whisper your safe word in Rico's ear."

Angie stiffened and looked at Jared.

"It's a safety measure. Rico is here to make sure if you use your safe word, all play stops until you indicate you're ready to start again."

"You mean..." Heat rose to her face. "He's going to listen to us?"

"My monitors are discreet, Angie," Gabe said. "Their job is to protect you in case your partner gets out of control. They listen for your safe word, otherwise, they ignore everything else they hear."

Angie took a deep breath and stepped up to Rico. He had to lean down so she could whisper "red" in his ear.

"Very good, ma'am." Rico smiled and opened the door.

Gabe glanced at his watch. "As we agreed, Jared, I'll be back at nine. Two hours from now." With that, he turned and walked away.

Jared guided her into the room and shut the door behind them. The room was close to what they had in their playroom. Her nerves danced in time with her heart. His arms encircled her waist, and he pulled her against him.

"Get your questions out of the way before we start."

Dang, it was like he could read her mind. "Explain the different floors to me, please."

"As Gabe said, the first floor is green for novices, for those who are starting off exploring the BDSM lifestyle, or simply because they want a private place to have sex."

"I see." Jared loosened his hold, and she slipped away. She wanted to explore more of the room while they talked. It would help calm her nerves. "This floor?"

"For the more experienced, much like my playroom."

"The blue floor?"

"That is for those living the lifestyle and don't have their own equipment."

Angie paused at the large bed and trailed her fingers over the soft sheets before going over to the open wooden cabinets. "And the top floor?"

"For those who embrace sadism and masochism. It can be very intense."

A tremor shook her body. "Have you ever used the top floor?"

"No." He crossed to her side and, with gentle fingers, lifted her chin up until he could gaze into her eyes. "I'm not into pain. Gabe allows it here because a submissive knows they're totally safe here."

"Because there are men like Rico outside the door?" She was still a little nervous about that.

"Yes. Gabe is able to keep his members safe because of monitors like Rico. If the safe word is uttered, he'll walk into the room to make sure the Dom has heard the word and to make sure the Dom has stopped."

"So no one is allowed into a room without a monitor?"

"Yes."

"This might sound crass but Gabe must be worth a fortune."

Jared laughed. "Gabe made his fortune in the tech world. He bought this place at auction years ago. It was an old hotel and he remodeled it."

"This is a hobby for him?"

"In a way. He wanted to give people a safe place to enjoy themselves, like at the ranch we wanted to give people a place to learn and play."

"I see. I interrupted you, I'm sorry."

"No worries. To continue, all subs must have a safe word to enter the room. Even Doms have them. And you saw the men at the entrance to the stairs."

"I did."

"Gabe or any of his managers are the only ones that can escort people to the rooms."

"Makes sense. Is everyone here a couple?"

"Unlike the ranch, no. Many members are single. They may have a single Dom or sub they play with."

"Okay." She could understand that. As a single person, if she was interested in the lifestyle, this would be a way to explore in a safe environment. But she couldn't see herself being here without Jared. "I have one more question."

"Go for it."

"One of the women downstairs was wearing a choker; it looked like it was made of tiny metal hearts. At first, I thought it was just a nice necklace, but the man she was with kept stroking it."

"It was probably a collar."

Angie tilted her head. "I don't understand."

"It's a sign between the Dom and sub of a committed relationship. In the community, it means the couple has accepted each other, kinks and all, for who they are."

She tucked the information away in the back of her brain. But not before her heart leapt at the thought of Jared giving her a collar.

"I want you to know, Gabe knows your limits and, of course, your safe words. If anything bothers you— and I mean *anything*—say your safe words. This is for your pleasure. And I want you to enjoy it."

"I want you to have your pleasure as well." Her fingers curved around his neck. She wanted him to enjoy this as much as she was. And when their time was up, maybe he wouldn't leave her.

"I'll have my pleasure, especially watching you come when Gabe and I fuck you."

Her heart jumped, and her body trembled at his words.

Jared's arms tightened around her. "If you don't want this to happen, Angie. It's okay. We can play without Gabe. This is your fantasy."

Angie bit her lip and then took a deep breath. "I want this. I want you to dominate me in every way." She did. She trusted Jared, and if she was honest with herself, she was falling in love with him.

It sounded crazy. This man did things to her body, but also to her emotions that she'd never felt in her entire life. It had been a long time since she'd felt so safe. If ever.

Jared grinned. "Ready?"

A thrill of pleasure shot though Angie. "One more question. How long are we going to play?" She'd noticed their bags by the door.

"All night."

***

Several hours later, Angie turned her head from where it rested on Jared's chest. They'd played for several hours before Jared carried her to the bed and told her to rest. Her body still hummed from Jared's attention.

She heard the door open and turned her head to see Gabe enter the room.

"Hey, Gabe," Jared said. "Sweetheart, are you still okay for the threesome?"

"Yes."

Gabe grinned and crossed the room to pick up a straight-back chair and set it in the middle of the room. Gabe stood on the chair and reached up to undo something on the ceiling.

"What is that?" she asked.

"A swing," Gabe answered.

She frowned. "It doesn't look like one."

Jared's laughter warmed her from the inside out. "It's a sex swing. We haven't used the one in my play room."

"Oh." After all this time with Jared, he could still surprise her.

Gabe sauntered to the bed with two bottles. "Your pleasure or mine?"

"You do her breasts, and I'll do her pussy." Jared sat up and snagged one of the bottles from Gabe while cradling her against his chest. "Lie back, baby, and let us take care of you."

"Okay." She laid on her back and opened her legs. Jared coated his fingers and parted her labia. She groaned.

"Baby?"

"Sensitive." It didn't surprise her, Jared had enjoyed using toys on her, keeping her on edge. "My nipples are too."

"This will make it better," Jared said.

"Why don't I believe that?" There was laugher in her voice as the men caressed her breasts and pussy with whatever was in the bottle. Her amusement turned to need. "You're using that warming cream, aren't you?"

"Yep," Jared said, and Gabe grinned.

"It is warming cream," Gabe said. "With something special." Gabe blew on her nipple.

Angie almost shot off the bed. What the hell was that? When he blew on her nipple, it felt like a thousand tiny prickles.

"It's working." The amusement in Jared's voice wasn't hard to miss.

"Time to play with her sexy ass." Gabe opened a different bottle.

She breathed in relief as she saw the bottle was just lube.

"Move with me." Jared put his arms around her and then he maneuvered their bodies, until she lay on top of him. His palms caressed her ass before dipping between them and pulling her ass cheeks open.

Angie took a breath as Gabe began to use the lube on her. Gabe's fingers weren't as big as Jared's, but she was becoming more aroused. The warming cream was doing its job. Her entire body throbbed with anticipation as Jared sat up with her in his arms.

Gabe lifted her away from Jared and set her on her feet. Jared joined them, and the two men led her over to the swing. She eyed it, trying to figure it out.

"Don't worry. We'll help you into it," Jared said.

"Why not use the bed?" she asked.

"This will allow Jared and me more control," Gabe commented.

"Plus, you won't have to worry about supporting yourself. The swing is built for this. No worries about your legs hurting, or your arms." Jared lifted her while Gabe guided her into the swing.

"It also gives us the ability to touch you as we fuck you silly." Gabe adjusted her legs in the straps, then buckled everything around her body.

Angie looked down. Her body was fully supported. There was a wide strip running under her ass, her legs secured and held wide open by more straps. She was tilted slightly forward, but not enough for her to feel unsafe. There was also a strap around her waist.

Jared nudged her, and she rocked. Angie squealed.

"Another advantage." Jared's eyes twinkled with mischief, and she knew she was in for the ride of her life with these two. It didn't bother her at all. She wanted this.

Jared moved in front of her and pressed his forehead against hers, gazing into her eyes. "I want you to talk to us. We need to hear you. We need to be sure this is pleasurable for you as it will be for us."

"You've done this before?" She'd known he was Becca's third.

"Only twice, once with Tyler and Becca, which you know about. And once here at the club with another member looking for a third."

"And Gabe?" She looked at him.

"Many times—with both men and women."

"Men…" Her eyes widened, and her mouth dropped open. She'd never thought of that.

"Yes." Gabe tapped her chin. "Women aren't the only ones who like a good ass fucking, and men want a threesome with another man."

"I never thought about it."

"Ah, but don't forget there are all sexual orientations in the lifestyle," Gabe said, his voice gentle.

"Right." She mentally chastised herself for falling down the rabbit hole of misconceptions. Now it all made sense.

Jared leaned over, his breath brushing her skin. "I'd rather fuck you all day than have two women."

Her heart leapt, and hot tendrils of desire swept through her. Did Jared have feelings for her? She pushed the thought away. This wasn't the time to analyze her relationship with him.

Gabe moved out of her sight, and a few moments later, his chest brushed her back as his hand covered her breasts. When had he undressed?

"Beautiful breasts, nice rosy ones, not too big and not too small." Gabe pinched her nipples. "Always ready to be played with."

Before she could think of anything to say, his palms skimmed over her abdomen. Jared placed his hands on her spread thighs, his hard cock brushing against her slit.

Gabe's fingers touched the top of her mound, then past her clit, to her pussy. He held her labia open, and the head of Jared's cock penetrated her.

"Oh, yes." She tried to shift her hips forward.

"Easy." Jared told her. "Let us do the work. You can play later." He thrust until half of his cock was buried in her.

Gabe tweaked her clit, making her gasp. The men laughed. "So responsive," Gabe said.

"My body is on fire."

"The cream is doing its job. We want you hot and wanting," Jared said as Gabe moved behind her. Angie jumped when Gabe caressed her ass.

"Wrap your legs around my waist," Jared commanded.

She hooked her ankles around Jared's back. More lube was massaged into her ass. Angie had expected more foreplay before they took her, but then again, she was primed and ready. Jared had made sure of that before Gabe's arrival.

Gabe's body heat stroked her skin, and his condom-covered cock touched her ass. Angie jumped at the contact.

"Easy, baby," Jared crooned. "You're ready for us."

"Yes." *Was that my voice?* It was so needy. Well, she was needy. Anticipation thrummed through her. Jared's arms encircled her, then his hands were on her ass, pulling her cheeks apart.

Jared's scent filled her. Sandalwood, pine, and sweat. Her nerves settled down. He was here with her; nothing would happen she didn't want. Gabe's cock was hard against her ass. Angie took a deep breath and pressed out.

Her mouth fell open as Gabe pushed into her. Hell, he was as big as Jared and was stretching her. There was a slight burning sensation as he moved. More lube was added.

"Talk to us, baby." Jared's breath brushed over her cheek.

Angie caught her breath. "You're both rock-hard inside me. I know Gabe isn't fully in yet." She sucked in a breath as Gabe moved. "I never knew it could feel like this."

"Like what?" Jared's lips caressed her neck.

"So good. I feel so full and..." She sucked in another breath. "So erotic."

Jared's grin against her skin caused her to smile. Gabe pulled out and pushed back in.

"Did you have to pick someone as big as you are?" She panted. She wanted to enjoy every minute of this, so that meant remembering to breathe.

"I could have picked someone bigger."

Angie snorted. "Right, like there's anyone bigger than you two."

Gabe's hot breath brushed over the back of her neck. "You're so fucking tight. You ass is gripping me hard."

Gabe flexed his hips, and Angie lifted her hips as if to impale herself on him. Jared's cock pushed farther into her. More. She wanted more. This was moving too slowly. Her body was on fire.

"You're killing me." She couldn't take much more of this. She needed them inside her. "Gabe, move, please."

"I don't want to hurt you." The strain in his voice was apparent.

"You won't. I need you to shift so I can take more of Jared." These two had to know how she felt. They'd done this before.

Gabe thrust into her, and she impaled herself on Jared. A cry left her lips as a tear slipped from her eye.

"Baby?" Jared's voice was filled with concern. "Gabe, pull out."

"No." She panted. "I'm okay." Her pussy adjusted around Jared. "Want Gabe fully in me. I want to feel full."

Jared slipped his arms around her back and cradled her body against his. "Do it."

Gabe gave another thrust, and she cried out again. Both men held still as her body adjusted around them.

"I'm full of you both." She couldn't stop trying to catch her breath. Two hot, sweaty bodies pressed against hers and them all connected. "So hard, so big, so male." Angie dropped her head against Jared's shoulder. His lips caressed her temple.

"So beautiful," Jared whispered. "Tell us when you're ready for us to move."

"We won't fuck you until you're ready," Gabe said, his breath brushing over her back, his palms resting on her hips.

Angie's body throbbed in the most pleasant way as she adjusted to having two men in her. She took a few deep breaths and said, "I'm ready."

"You call the shots," Jared said.

Her pussy muscles tightened as Jared pulled back, then he pushed in as Gabe drew back. "Oh my goodness." She could feel them both; it was so strange, yet so satisfying. "Can you feel each other's cocks?"

"Yes," both men said together.

"How does that feel?" She wanted to know what they were feeling. Was it the same tingling sensations she felt?

"Fantastic," Gabe commented, his harsh breathing against her skin as his lips caressed her shoulder.

"Sweetheart." Jared leaned his forehead against hers, their gazes connecting. "Your sweet pussy keeps tightening around my cock. Gabe's dick is making the ride so much tighter, sweeter, and knowing you're enjoy this makes it worth everything."

Her lips found his and their tongues tangled together. This man was making her fantasy come true. Jared broke the kiss, then kissed her cheeks. There was love and caring in those kisses.

The two men moved in tandem, and with each stroke, her body grew warmer. Her need grew stronger. There were flutters in her belly, and they were starting to fill her body. "Please, faster." Her mouth was dry, but she didn't want to stop. She wanted this for herself, for them.

"Okay." Jared took her mouth once again, kissing her hard and deep. Angie had to tear her mouth away so she could breathe.

"Talk to us," Jared commanded.

"I don't know what to say. My body is on fire. I can feel you both pumping in and out of me, but I also know you're both being careful not to hurt me."

"We won't." Gabe's labored tone floated over her shoulder.

Angie gazed into Jared's eyes. "Take me the way you want to."

Hesitation floated in Jared's eyes. His hands tightened on her hips.

She licked her lips. "Do it. Take me, make me come, show me what it means to belong to you."

Heat flared in his gaze. Jared inhaled and nodded. Gabe slipped his hands over Jared's on her hips. They anchored her and then they began to thrust, harder and faster. Angie's eyes fluttered shut.

With each thrust, their strength overwhelmed her. Their power was incredible, but there was tenderness as well. Her body was taking them. Her body shook with need.

"Let it go, baby," Jared said. "Let yourself fly over the cliff; we'll catch you."

"I can't." She was afraid of the unknown hanging in front of her. She quivered.

"You can." Gabe's hands slipped from her hips to her breasts and squeezed. "Come for us, Angie."

She shook her head, even though everything inside her was climbing higher and higher. She could only allow it to happen. Gabe slid his hand from her breast, then used his fingernail to play with her clit.

She tightened around the two men as her climax hit. They didn't stop. They kept going, building the fire higher and higher. They were all going to burn up. Gabe teased her clit again.

The second climax only intensified her passion. She needed more. She wanted more. Angie tried to move, but she had no traction. They way the men held her, she could barely move. "More, I need more." She couldn't believe those words left her mouth. Oh god, they moved faster—she didn't know how—and their cocks were swelling within her.

"Now," Jared said.

Angie screamed when Gabe pinched her clit, causing another climax. This one hit with the force of a tornado sweeping through the room. Her body thrashed around them, then the men shouted and slammed into her one last time.

Jared's hot climax fill her pussy and Gabe pulsing in her ass. The men held her between them. Angie had no idea how long they stayed that way. Gabe was the first to move. He slipped from her ass.

"Gabe?" Jared asked.

"I'm okay." Gabe's panting reached Angie's ears. "Give me a minute."

"Open your eyes, sweetheart." Jared's soft voice had her opening her eyes. He was staring down at her. "You are so perfect." He gave her a soft kiss.

Her arms tightened around his neck. She didn't even know when she'd put them there, and her hips shifted.

"Easy." Jared's fingers tightened on her hips. "Don't move, sweetheart." He withdrew from her pussy, causing a minor climax. Angie realized she felt empty, but so satisfied.

"Let's get you out of this," Jared said.

Within minutes, Gabe and Jared had her out of the swing and on the bed where both men cuddled her. Her body was sated, and loved. That was probably an odd thing to think, but that was the only thing that fit. Her love for Jared filled her.

"You are fantastic, Angie." Gabe's lips touched her cheek. "Thank you for allowing me to be a partner in your pleasure."

Angie smiled as her lashes fluttered shut. She'd rest for a while and then see what other trouble they could get into.

✳✳✳

Jared kept his gaze on Angie as Gabe climbed off the bed and walked into the attached bathroom. Angie was sound asleep.

He was still in shock that she'd urged them to take her the way they wanted. Never once did she utter her safe word, and from the expression on her face, she'd thoroughly enjoyed her first and last threesome.

That was if he had anything to say about it. He tried to rein in his thoughts, but he couldn't. Angie had found a way into his hardened heart, and he didn't want to let her go. But she wasn't his to keep.

Their agreement was for two weeks. Sunday, she'd head back to San Francisco and that would be the end of it. But it didn't have to be. He could probably find a way to bring her up to the ranch on weekends. After all, Becca was her best friend.

He wanted more than a weekend relationship. He just wasn't sure how to make that happen. Jared yawned.

"Take a nap, my friend," Gabe said, coming out of the bathroom fully dressed. "The room is yours until morning."

"What time is it?"

Gabe looked at his watch. "Almost midnight."

Jared blinked. "Midnight?" He hadn't expected it to be that late. Even though they had rested a bit before Gabe joined them, he and Gabe had enjoyed Angie's body for almost three hours. Jared's arms tightened around Angie.

"She's absolutely perfect for you, my friend. She's adventurous, responsive, and sexy. And most of all, she understands your needs and desires." Gabe walked to the door, and before he opened it, he looked back. "You are a lucky man. Thank you for sharing her with me, and make sure you keep her. She will make you happy."

Before Jared could reply, Gabe shut the door behind him. Jared relaxed against the pillows. Yes, he was a lucky man. But only for one more day unless they tried the weekend relationship thing. At least he'd see her then. One day, their relationship might end, but it didn't have to be now.

All I have to do is ask her.

Was that a risk he was willing to take?

Chapter Eleven

♥

They drove back from Sacramento on Saturday morning, and then spent the day lazing around, just chatting and holding each other. He wanted to give her time to recover. And last night, they'd made love.

These last two weeks were special to him, but he could never forget who he was and what his needs were. While Angie had enjoyed herself, he was aware that it would be hard for her to have a lifetime of his version of sex. But he hadn't asked her either.

He would always want his sex on the rougher side, the wilder side, and no woman wanted that full-time. He'd learned his lesson when his ex-fiancée walked out—but not before explaining that his controlling nature was why she was leaving and now she understood why all his previous relationships failed.

He wasn't asking Angie for a lifetime. That was true, but even if they did a weekend relationship, deeper feelings could be established, and he'd eventually break her heart and his.

Jared couldn't do that to Angie. He cared too much for her. *No, it's better this way.* He'd miss her, not just for sex, but for companionship and having a work partner who understood.

And now, Sunday morning had arrived faster than he wanted. He gazed at a sleeping Angie. Could he let her go? He hadn't come up with a plan for asking her to stay. He wasn't a coward, but her rejection would hurt, and part of that was why he couldn't ask her.

Angie snuggled closer as if sensing his thoughts. He glanced down.

"Good morning, sweetheart." Still drowsy, she wiggled her body against his. He leaned over and brushed her lips with his. In a few hours she would be gone, and the past two weeks would be a memory he'd carry forever.

"Morning." She drew her fingers from his chest down to his groin and cupped his dick. She stroked him from base to tip, and all coherent thoughts left his mind.

"Keep that up and we won't get out of bed."

"Sounds good to me." Angie leaned over and licked one of his nipples and then the other one.

"Witch." He rolled her onto her back and started making slow sweet love to her. It might be their last time together, and he was going to make it special and make it last.

***

Angie zipped her suitcase shut. She didn't want to leave. She didn't want to go back to a job where she had to make all the decisions for everyone. The city was going to feel empty without her best friend, and she wanted to stay with Jared.

But he hadn't asked her, and she couldn't ask him and deal with the rejected when he said no. Especially since he'd never indicated he wanted their relationship to go more than the two weeks. Her heart was breaking, but she had to accept it.

Jared's not into long-term relationships.

She'd agreed to the Dom/sub arrangement and to the two weeks to explore. Their two weeks were done. Angie glanced around her room. She was going to miss these comfortable peach walls, the large bed, and having Jared next to her at night. Lord, this hurt more than she expected.

"Ready?"

Turning, she saw Jared leaning against the doorway. "Yes." What else could she say?

He walked in and picked up her suitcase. There was nothing in his actions that told her he wanted her to stay. No, he was very closed down. His expression and body language revealed nothing. She walked out of the room and down the staircase with heavy feet and heart.

Once outside, the bright sunshine didn't warm her as it usually did. Her car had been brought around to the front of the ranch house. Jared placed her bag in the trunk and slammed the lid shut. Angie jumped at the noise. It was too quiet.

Probably because the construction was finished. Angie couldn't believe how much work had been done while she was here. She wanted to stay and explore. Maybe she'd come back one weekend and visit Becca so she could see everything. See Jared one more time.

Strong arms snagged her around the waist, and she was drawn against Jared's hard body. She glanced up at him. He lowered his head. His lips took hers in a kiss. It wasn't a gentle good-bye kiss; it was one of possession, of passion.

Hope filled her as they kissed. Maybe he needed physical contact to ask her to stay. Because if he asked, she'd stay in a heartbeat. She was invested in him. Jared lifted his head.

"Have a safe drive." He rested his forehead against hers.

"I will."

Ask me, Jared. Please.

"Behave yourself when you get back to San Francisco." He swatted her ass.

"Of course." Her hands tightened on his shoulders. His little swat heated her blood like no one else ever had. "I love you." The words slipped out before she could prevent them.

Jared's eyes widened before his face went completely blank. "You can't," he whispered, before he pulled away from her and walked away.

Tears filled her eyes as he kept his back to her. How could he walk away like that? It was just like their beginning. He was abandoning her. She closed her eyes to keep the tears from falling, then fumbled for the door handle of her car.

Go. After. Him.

But she couldn't. No, it was over. He didn't want her. She started the engine and put the car into gear. She wouldn't chase him. If he didn't want her, so be it.

Angie drove away from the ranch house slowly, but Jared was nowhere in sight. She managed to wait until she was twenty miles from the ranch to pull over and cry. Best to get it out now and then drive home.

She cried for the little girl abandoned by her parents, all the foster families that sent her back, for her adopted family who, while they loved her, didn't quite know how to help her, and most of all, for Jared.

The only man who'd captured her heart only to refuse it.

Her life was never going to be the same.

Chapter Twelve

♥

Monday morning.

Angie strode into her office. This place was worse than hell. When she arrived home last night, she dropped her suitcase, climbed into bed, and cried, then cried some more. She couldn't seem to stop.

Finally, she climbed out of bed, took a hot shower, made herself some soup, and curled up on the sofa and watched a sappy movie so she could cry without feeling guilty. It had taken her twice the time this morning to conceal her tear-ravaged face.

She looked at her desk and felt like crying again. It was piled high with work. *Did no one do* anything *while I was gone?* As she blew out a breath between pursed lips, she sat and turned on her computer. The company logo swam before her eyes.

No more crying. Hadn't she cried enough? Forcing the tears away, she began sorting out the piles on her desk. Then she turned to her computer and opened her task manager app. While she laid awake and stared at the ceiling, she started making priority lists in her head.

First task: Resign from her job. She hated this job. She'd only stayed out of a sense of duty.

Well, screw that.

She ignored her full inbox and began typing.

Second task: *I'm going back to the ranch and confront Jared.*

How dare he ignore her love for him? She wasn't ready to give up on him yet. There had to be a reason he walked away from her, and she was going to find out what it was. She was going to get her man, even if it meant giving up her pride to do it.

Jared made her feel whole, wanted, and sexy. She wasn't going to give that up. She needed him. She loved him, even if he didn't love her. Angie was determined to be with him. On his terms, if need be. But if a relationship with Jared was impossible—for whatever reason—she would at least have closure. And closure was better than not knowing.

"Well, well, well, if it isn't Miss Ice Queen back from her vacation."

Angie glanced up to see Bill from customer service step into her office. *Great, I have to deal with this idiot today.* "I really don't have time for your issues today, Bill."

"Oh yes, you do." He gave her a slimy grin, and she shivered.

What a contrast from Jared's grin. Jared's made her wet. "As you can see, I have a ton of work." She gestured to the files on her desk. Not that she was planning to do much today.

"Don't worry; this won't take long." He pushed the door shut behind him.

***

Jared followed the receptionist's instructions to Angie's office. Outside the closed door, he took a deep breath. *I should kick my own ass for letting her drive away.*

When she blew his mind with her words of love, his instincts kicked in, and he walked away from her. He was an idiot. After he made it back inside the ranch house, he knew he'd made a mistake, but by the time he got back outside, she was gone.

He'd spent last night doing some long hard thinking. He'd been a coward not to ask her to stay. Angie's words of love were honest and true. She wasn't like his child-hood sweethearts, his college girlfriends, or his ex-fiancée.

No, Angie said the words because she meant them, not because she thought he wanted to hear them. Unlike the women of his past, Angie loved him for who he was. She enjoyed his domination and his need for sex. And instead of embracing her love, he walked away, giving in to the old tapes playing in his head.

Therapist, heal thy self.

Jared wasn't going to walk away now. He would make this up to her, show her that he was a man worthy of her love.

And, yes, he loved her.

He had for a while, but he'd been too blind to recognize it for what it was. He wouldn't let Angie down this time. He raised his arm to knock when he heard the raised voices.

"I don't have time for your crap today." Angie's voice. Jared heard the frustration but also the exhaustion.

"I saw you at Xavier's on Friday," a male voice said.

Jared swore silently. Who was this man? The last thing he wanted was to endanger Angie's work. Besides Xavier's had a very strict NDA.

"So?" Angie's voice was strong. Go girl.

"Angie, my dear. This is a conservative company. What do you think the higher-ups would say about finding out you went to a BDSM club?"

Jared was beginning to hate this guy. Plus, he had to find out who he was so Gabe could expel him for violation of the NDA.

"What's to stop me from telling them about *you* being there? And notifying the club that you confronted me in violation of the NDA?"

There was his Angie. The fighter.

"Ah, but you didn't see me, did you? You were too wrapped up in your pretty little man and his friend. It really doesn't matter, you see, because you're going to do everything I tell you to do. And if you don't..." The man gave a cruel laugh. "I'll make your life a living hell."

Jared's anger overflowed. This little weasel was trying to blackmail his woman. Oh, *hell* no. *Time to put an end to this.* He turned the knob and started to open the door.

"Bill, go fuck yourself."

Jared barely held back his laughter.

"I'm my own woman, and I'll decide who my Dom is, and it isn't you. Now, run along, I have work to do." Her tone was dismissive.

"You won't have a job. I'll make sure you're fired."

"Doesn't matter. I've already emailed my resignation. Now, get the hell out of my office."

She quit her job? Why? It couldn't be because of this man and his threats?

"You'll never get another job as a CPA."

That was enough. Jared strode into her office. "She already has another job with my company."

Bill turned, his jaw dropped open, and his face paled.

"Bill, is it?" Jared started. "I heard everything you said. Expect a call today from Xavier's revoking your membership followed by a lawsuit for harassment of a member and breaking your NDA."

Angie's expression was a mixture of surprise and relief. "Yes, go, Bill. I'll be calling HR and reporting you as well."

Bill glared at Angie for a moment, before skirting around Jared and leaving the office.

"Alone at last." Jared walked over to Angie and pulled her into his arms. "I'm sorry I walked away. I want you in my arms and in my life."

"Jared—"

"*Shhh.*" He brushed his lips against hers. "Let me get this out. I walked away from you yesterday, and that was the biggest mistake in my life. One I will never make again." He gazed into her eyes. "You surprised me when you said you loved me."

"Why did you walk away?"

"I've had other women tell me that they love me, but the minute they understand I like my sex kinky and frequently, they leave."

"Are they crazy?"

Jared grinned. "I don't know. I was engaged for a while."

Angie's eyes grew wide. "What happened?"

"She said she loved me and didn't mind that I like my sex a little different. But when I showed her what I liked and wanted, she lost it and told me I was a freak. I never saw her again."

"You're not a freak." Angie curved her fingers around his neck. Her warmth making him feel better. "How long ago was this?"

"Six years."

"She scarred you."

"Yes. Yesterday, I didn't know how to respond to you. Today, I do. I love you, Angie. Come back to the ranch with me. Be my accountant, my lover, my everything."

Angie froze in his embrace. Jared fought back his insecurities. He wouldn't force her to do anything, that wasn't him. This had to be her decision, but his heart hurt at the thought of her refusing. Also, he would use every trick in his arsenal to make her agree.

"I have one question."

"Yes."

"Will you be my Dom?"

Relief poured through Jared. "Forever." He lifted her onto her desk. "Stay there."

He closed the door and flipped the lock.

***

Angie's heart pounded. *Jared loves me.* She almost thought she was dreaming. While some women might say he needed to grovel more, Angie didn't want that. Jared was a proud man, but he'd come to her. Her Dom bared his heart to her.

"Strip off your panties."

His words sent a shaft of excitement through her. Thank goodness she wore a skirt today. She wiggled on her desk until she got her panties off and dangled them from her finger.

Jared stalked over, and she couldn't stop smiling. He pulled her off the desk and onto her feet. He took her panties, wadded them up, and placed them in his pocket. Then he took her hand and dropped to one knee.

Angie trembled. *Oh. My. God.*

"Angie Davidson, you are the love of my life, the only woman who has ever understood me and loves me for the way I am. Will you be my wife?"

"But...it's only been two weeks."

"I knew what I wanted the moment I saw you at the ranch. You. It just took my brain longer to catch up. I want you forever."

Tears filled Angie's eyes. Happy tears. She had to clear her throat before she could speak. "Yes, I'll marry you. I love you so much."

Jared rose to his feet and pulled something from his pocket. "In a few days, we can go get a ring to match this."

She stared at the diamond choker in his hand. Jared's words about what a choker meant in the lifestyle came back to her. "But how?"

"There are some very good jewelry stores in San Francisco." He fastened the choker around her neck.

A sense of peace and love flowed over Angie. "I'm never taking this off." She threw her arms around his neck. "Now, take me home to our playroom."

"Anything my love wants." He swept her into his arms and carried her out of her office.

***

Thank you for reading Tangled Temptation. The companion story Broken Rules (Tyler and Becca's book) was released in May and you can grab it at your favorite ebook vendor. You can also grab it from my direct sale store on my website: www.marietuhart.com

Coming in August will me the first book One Wicked Weekend in my new series Fantasies Inc., will release. In October Decoding Emma the second book will release. To keep up-to-date you can join my newsletter at: https://www.marietuhart.com/join-mailing-list.html

***

Preview of One Wicked Weekend

❤

Marcus

I sat back in my chair as Cassie Adams marched into my office, her blue eyes flashing with displeasure. I fought to wipe the smug grin off my face. Finally, some emotion out of her. Satisfaction flowed through my body. Cassie was ready to do battle, all buttoned up with her hair pulled back. Earlier in the day, her hair had been down and two buttons undone. I noticed. I notice everything where she's concerned.

Maybe she was shoring up her defenses. It didn't matter to me. She was mine now.

My intimate gift had the desired effect—her in my office. It didn't escape my notice that she waited until everyone left for lunch to confront me. "Good afternoon, Cassie." I kept my tone even.

"Don't 'good afternoon' me, Marcus DeLuca. I've had enough. This has got to stop and stop now." She stood before my desk, vibrating with what I wanted to believe was unfulfilled desire, but I knew better. She was also irritated.

It didn't matter. She was here.

I'd picked my latest gift with care and the knowledge it would probably push her over the edge, right where I wanted her. I leaned farther back in my leather executive chair to ease the pressure in my groin. "What has to stop?"

I held my amusement in when she stomped her foot and a storm kicked up in those baby blues of hers. It took all my control not to jump out of my chair, push her over my desk, and fuck her. She did that to me—made me lose control—and I didn't like it. I prided myself on my iron-tight control.

"Don't play games with me. The flowers, the notes, and the gifts. It stops now."

The time for teasing was over. She'd thrown down the challenge, and I planned to pick it up. "I made my intentions clear two months ago. I told you the gloves were coming off, and I was going to pursue you until you gave in." I'd made a habit of studying her, to see what made her tick so I could make her mine.

She'd never told me no. I'd respect her wishes if she did. But I suspected she didn't want to and had no idea how to deal with me. Sexual chemistry had arced between us from the first day we first met. I wanted her like I'd wanted no other woman, and I was determined to have her.

"Yes, but..." Her gaze dropped to her feet, a delicate flush coloring her cheeks.

A flash of tenderness welled up in me at her indecision—along with the need to pull her into my arms and comfort her. But at the same time, I wanted to kiss her until she couldn't breathe and fuck her until she screamed my name.

"I can't take this anymore." Her voice was whisper soft, but I heard the words as clear as if she'd shouted them.

My cock jumped. I would prove to her that I was more than just a co-worker, and I planned to show her a relationship between us could work. "What are you willing to give me to stop?"

Her head snapped up, and she gnawed on her lower lip. "Twenty-four hours."

"Not enough. A hundred and twenty." I was willing to negotiate with her, but she wasn't going to get everything her way.

Her mouth opened and then closed. Her gaze darted left, then right, before settling back on my face. I could almost see the wheels turning in her head, trying to figure out her next move.

"Too long. Forty-eight."

I stood and crossed to her. I needed to be close to her as we negotiated this agreement. Little did she know it was only temporary. "Still not enough. Ninety-six uninterrupted hours with you."

Her nose scrunched and her lashes swept down, cutting off my view of her very expressive eyes. "Sixty. From six Friday night until six Monday morning."

I noted the stubborn set of her chin. It wasn't an ideal bargain, but I could live with it. I would not fail in winning her over. Leaning close, I whispered, "I'll take it."

Cassie exhaled, lashes rising until our gazes clashed. "What are the ground rules?"

"There are none."

Her eyes widened. I had her now, and I wasn't letting her go. I held her gaze, my tone hard and commanding. "No barriers. No rules."

Her shoulders dipped, then straightened as if she was preparing for battle. "All right, but when the sixty hours are done, we're finished. I mean it. No flowers, no gifts, no mention of the weekend. Ever."

Without another word, she spun on her heels to leave my office. I hurried across the room and captured her by the shoulders before she made it to the door. I leaned over, my lips brushing her ear, and smelled her fresh scent. "Remember what I said at the party."

Her swift intake of breath was my answer. She did remember.

"You belong to me," I whispered.

"I belong to no man."

I slid my hands down her arms past her clenched fists and encircled her waist, pulling her flush against my body. She didn't struggle, but her breathing grew choppy. I pressed my erect dick against her ass. "You will belong to me, I promise."

"For sixty hours only." She wrenched herself from my embrace and turned her head to glare at me. "That's all you'll get, Marcus. That's all it can be."

"I wouldn't bet on it."

"There are sexual harassment laws you have to abide by."

"Only if you file." A smug smile crossed my lips.

"I will if you make one move toward me after the weekend." Pivoting, she marched out of my office, treating me to her luscious ass as she walked away.

I closed my office door and locked it before returning to my chair. I gently released my zipper and pulled my cock out. It was hard and pulsing. Soon, I'd have Cassie beneath me and then she'd learn the type of man I am.

About the author

♥

Marie Tuhart lives in the beautiful Pacific Northwest with her two dogs, Tommy and Trina. Marie brings to life contemporary approachable alpha heroes and the spunky women who take them to task. Her high-heat, emotional books, many with BDSM elements, inviting the reader to slid the silky scarves between their fingers, fell the kiss of a flogger on their flesh in breathless anticipation of what or who will come next. Embrace the temptation and enjoy a happily ever after that's always about the heroine.

Check out Marie's website at: https://www.marietuhart.com

Other Books by Marie Tuhart

♥

Tempt (Wicked Sanctuary Series)

Entice (Wicked Sanctuary Series)

Seduce (Wicked Sanctuary Series)

Ravish (Wicked Sanctuary Series)

Possess (Wicked Sanctuary Series)

Tantalize (Wicked Sanctuary Series)

Edged (Wicked Sanctuary Series)

Unmasked (Wicked Sanctuary Series)

Too Hot (Wicked Sanctuary Series)

Wicked Sanctuary Novellas:

Untamed

Power Play

Claiming Rose

Standalone Books:

Embracing Desire

Broken Rules

Tangled Temptation

www.ingramcontent.com/pod-product-compliance
Lightning Source LLC
Chambersburg PA
CBHW040526170726
48295CB00012B/348